Kayaks and Killers

Sapphire Beach Cozy Mystery Series
(Book 8)

Angela K. Ryan

John Paul Publishing

TEWKSBURY, MASSACHUSETTS

Angela K. Ryan
John Paul Publishing
Post Office Box 283
Tewksbury, MA 01876

Publisher's Note: This is a work of fiction. Names, characters, places, and incidents are a product of the author's imagination. Locales and public names are sometimes used for atmospheric purposes. Any resemblance to actual people, living or dead, or to businesses, companies, events, institutions, or locales is completely coincidental.

Cover Design © 2020 MariahSinclair.com
Book Layout © 2017 BookDesignTemplates.com

Kayaks and Killers/ Angela K. Ryan. -- 1st ed.
ISBN: 978-1-7353064-3-8

A Note of Thanks from the Author

I would like to warmly thank all those who generously shared their time and knowledge in the research of this book, especially:

Jacki Strategos, Premier Sotheby's
International Realty, Marco Island

Carol Buccieri
Bella Stella Beads, Haverhill, Massachusetts

Marco Island Fire Rescue
Marco Island, Florida

Any errors are my own.

Chapter 1

CONNIE PETRETTA BURST out laughing at the flurry of excitement racing in her direction.

That flurry was Stephanie Harrison, who had become one of Connie's very best friends since she relocated from the Boston area to Sapphire Beach nearly two years ago. With every step, Stephanie's long athletic legs kicked up a pile of white silky sand, and her arms flailed as she ran toward Connie and her other bestie, Elyse Miller.

"What are you doing here so early?" Elyse asked, giggling at the sight.

"My 11:00 appointment was a no-show." Stephanie's broad smile indicated that she wasn't too disappointed. "Since Andrea was my only client for the day, I was able to come early." Stephanie was a physical therapist and worked for a company that provided in-home therapy.

"Wasn't this the client who insisted she couldn't meet you until 11:00?" Elyse asked.

"Yup," Stephanie said, settling into one of the lounge chairs that Connie had set up for herself and her friends. They had planned this beach day weeks ago, and each of them had taken the day off from work and their other responsibilities to make it happen. "I tried to schedule my only appointment of the day for earlier in the morning so I could get to the beach ASAP, but my client, Andrea, is on vacation this week and had plans earlier in the morning. I'll bet she was having so much fun on her first day of vacation that she completely forgot about her physical therapy appointment."

Connie smiled and shrugged. "Her loss is our gain."

"Nothing can bother me today," Stephanie said. "I'm here with my two best friends soaking up some rays on a Monday in late October and dipping my feet in the Gulf of Mexico. Life doesn't get any better than this."

Connie leaned back in her lounge chair and pressed her feet into the soft sand. Then she turned her face toward the sun and inhaled the warm, salty air. "I can't argue with that." Connie had been looking forward to spending this day with Stephanie and Elyse for weeks. Between Connie running her jewelry shop, Elyse's business as a realtor - not to mention her husband and two girls - and Stephanie's more-than-full-time job as a physical therapist, it was rare for the three women to have an entire day to spend together.

"You didn't miss a thing," Elyse said, lazily lifting her sunglasses. "We just got here, too."

Connie opened her large, blue cooler and pulled out three cans of cranberry-lime seltzer water. She handed one to each of her friends and opened the third for herself.

"I love your little setup, by the way," Stephanie said, gesturing toward Connie's stand-up paddleboard, which she had set in the middle of the lounge chairs as a makeshift coffee table.

It was a clever use for her paddleboard while it wasn't in the water, if Connie did say so herself.

Connie lifted her can of seltzer water. "It's too early for a real toast, but I thought we could raise a glass, or a can, just the same."

"What are we toasting?" Elyse asked.

"Us, of course. We've had a lot thrown at us in the past few months, and we persevered. That deserves a toast."

"In that case," Elyse said, raising her can, "here's to the successful purchases of the buildings that house *Just Jewelry* and Ruby's souvenir shop." Connie had been afraid that she, as well as her neighbor and friend, Ruby, would have to relocate their businesses, after their landlord announced he was selling his properties so he could retire worry-free. That might have meant that Connie and Ruby would have to move their businesses from the properties that had become like a second home. However, after Hurricane Emery swept through southwest Florida in late August, Connie's landlord dropped the price of both shops. This allowed Connie to purchase the building that housed her own store, and her parents, as an investment, purchased Ruby's shop. Elyse, being a realtor, handled the transactions.

4

"And to the completed repairs on Stephanie's bungalow and Connie's shop from the hurricane damage," Elyse added. "We all came through the storm better than we had hoped."

"Speaking of something being better than we could have hoped for, we should also toast Hurricane Emery for bringing Stephanie and Gallagher together," Connie added.

Gallagher owned *Gallagher's Tropical Shack*, a thatched-roofed restaurant and bar across the street from *Just Jewelry*, where Connie sold Fair Trade pieces, in addition to her own handmade creations. Gallagher and Stephanie started dating after getting to know one another while they were sheltered-in-place at Palm Paradise, which was the condominium building where Connie lived.

All three took a long drink from their cans.

"Speaking of Gallagher," Elyse said. "How *are* things going with him?"

Stephanie cheeks turned pink. But definitely not from the sun.

Elyse laughed. "That well, huh?"

Connie tapped the paddleboard with her palm. "Now that I see how happy the two of you are together, I could kick myself for not introducing you sooner."

Stephanie shook her head. "Don't feel badly. The timing of when we met was perfect. We've both been super busy over the past couple of years with our careers, and we were each starting to realize that something was missing from our lives when we met. I don't think either of us would have been ready for a relationship if we had met a year ago."

"I can tell you one thing for sure," Connie said. "Gallagher smiles a lot more. And he visits *Just Jewelry* more frequently than ever. He brings us complimentary smoothies and snacks, especially on the days Grace is working."

"You can't blame him for trying to get in good with his new girlfriend's mother," Elyse said. "Smart man."

Stephanie's mother, Grace Jenkins, was Connie's neighbor, friend, and part-time employee.

Stephanie smiled and blushed again.

"Okay, we'll leave you alone," Elyse said. "We're just so happy for you and Gallagher."

"By the way, Elyse," Stephanie said, "I gave Gallagher your phone number. He'll be calling you to set up an appointment to look at some houses. He was waiting to complete the hurricane repairs on his restaurant so he could see how much money would be left in his savings, but he's ready to get out of his beat up old trailer and into a grown-up's house, as he put it."

"I'll look forward to hearing from him." Elyse winked at Stephanie. "I'll try to direct him to a neighborhood near you."

Stephanie playfully tossed some sand in Elyse's direction. "You're impossible!"

Elyse raised her hands in mock surrender. "Okay, this time I mean it. I'm done teasing you. Let's move on to Connie and Zach," she said with a mischievous smile.

"That's right," Stephanie said. "I heard Zach's parents are coming to town to meet you."

"They're not coming to meet *me*," Connie said. "They are coming to visit their son. It was his mother's birthday a couple of weeks ago, so they are coming for a belated celebration."

"And to check out his girlfriend before the wedding," Elyse said.

This time, it was Connie who tossed some sand in Elyse's direction.

"Oh, come on. We all know it's only a matter of time before there's a wedding," Elyse said. "You two have been dating for nearly two years now, haven't you?"

"We met two years ago in January, but it's been less than a year that we've been serious."

"When you're in your mid-thirties like us, that's long enough to know," Elyse said.

"When are they arriving in town?" Stephanie asked.

"They fly in on Friday. We're all going to dinner that night."

"You see, the first thing Zach's doing with his parents is taking them to meet you," Elyse said.

"Stop. Don't make me more nervous than I already am."

"They're going to love you," Elyse said. "I've met Pauline and Ben before. They are great people."

Elyse's husband, Detective Joshua Miller, was also a detective, along with Connie's boyfriend, Detective Zachary Hughes, in the Sapphire Beach Police Department. So, Elyse had known Zach longer than she had known Connie. Connie hoped Elyse was right about Zach's parents.

"Not to change the subject, but I, for one, am thrilled that we have the entire day together," Stephanie said.

"Me, too." Elyse finished her seltzer water and threw the empty can back in the cooler. "Emma is going to a friend's house after school, and I don't have to pick Victoria up from daycare until 5:30. There's nothing like a relaxing day on the beach with your best friends."

"We need to do this more often," Stephanie added.

The women spent the next couple of hours soaking in the sun, bathing in the crystal blue water, and taking a leisurely walk on the beach. At about 12:30, they broke into the cooler and devoured the chicken salad sandwiches, chips, and cookies that Connie had packed for lunch.

While they were eating, Connie pointed to a lime-green kayak off in the distance that looked as if it were drifting toward the shore. "That kayaker has the right idea. He or she is lying back in the sun and floating the day away."

As they put their trash in the cooler to dispose of it later, the water was calling Connie's name. "My mom always told me to wait twenty minutes after eating before swimming, but patience has never been my strong suit. I'm going back in now."

Stephanie and Elyse followed Connie into the warm salt water until they were waist deep.

Like three little girls, the women rode the waves back to shore, then waded back out and did it again. After a while, they had drifted far from their lounge chairs, so they swam back to where they had started. It was easy to tell which lounge chairs belonged to them, because theirs were the only ones set up around a paddleboard coffee table.

Connie looked toward the horizon and noticed that the lime-green kayak they had seen earlier was still drifting toward them. Connie's gaze settled on the boat, rising and falling on the waves. An eerie feeling swept over her when she couldn't get a clear view of the kayaker.

Elyse glanced toward the kayak then back to Connie. "What is it? You look like something is wrong."

"It's just that I don't see a driver in that boat," Connie said.

At this point, the kayak was about twenty yards away. Elyse swam toward it, and when she arrived, she let out a shriek. Connie and Stephanie waited anxiously as Elyse pulled the kayak towards them. As it got closer, Connie realized the problem.

There was a woman lying in the kayak alright, but she wasn't sunbathing. She was dead.

When Stephanie saw the body, she let out a loud gasp. "Now I know why my 11:00 physical therapy appointment didn't show up. That's Andrea Fontaine, my client."

Chapter 2

CONNIE AND ELYSE stared dumbfounded at Stephanie.

"Are you *sure* that's your client?" Elyse asked.

Stephanie turned her head away from the body. "There's no doubt about it. That's Andrea."

Connie and Elyse dragged the kayak onto shore and out of reach of the crashing waves. Stephanie waded ahead of them and did her best to keep curious eyes away and to ensure that none of the children playing on the seashore happened upon the tragic scene.

Elyse darted over to her lounge chair and grabbed the beach bag sitting underneath. She pulled out her phone and walked back toward Connie and Stephanie while she called 9-1-1.

"She's just lying in the kayak," Elyse said to the operator. "It looks like she might have had a heart attack out on the water."

"I don't think it was a heart attack," Stephanie whispered to Connie. "She was one of the fittest forty-five-year-olds I know."

"Maybe she had some type of hidden heart condition," Connie suggested.

Stephanie ran her hand through her wavy brown hair. "I guess it's possible. I just can't believe she was out there all this time, and we didn't check the kayak. I just assumed the kayaker was taking a break from paddling to catch some rays. People do that all the time."

Connie glanced at Andrea's body. "She's been dead for a while, Stephanie. I don't think it would have mattered if we had found her any earlier."

Stephanie turned and stood with her back to the boat. "I can't look anymore. I'll never be able to get this image out of my head."

Connie placed her hand on Stephanie's shoulder. The shock was wearing off, and it suddenly occurred to her that they should cover the body out of respect. Connie went to get the beach towel off her lounge chair and said a silent prayer as she gently placed it over Andrea's body.

"Andrea was more than a client," Stephanie said. "She was a friend, too."

"I'm so sorry for your loss," Connie said. She gazed out toward the Gulf of Mexico, looking for the right words to comfort her friend when, in the distance, she noticed something she hadn't seen before. There was a second kayak, which was overturned, rising and falling on the waves. "Look," Connie said, pointing toward it. "Its blue color blends with the water, so I didn't notice it before. I have to get out there to see if someone needs help."

At this point, Elyse had finished her 9-1-1 call and was attempting to control the small crowd that was gradually gathering around the scene. Connie hoped the police would arrive before the curiosity factor became too difficult to manage.

Connie jogged to her paddleboard and threw the oar on top. Without even taking the time to put on her life vest, she dragged her board into the water, hopped on top, and paddled as fast as she could in the direction of the overturned kayak.

Connie hadn't used her paddleboard much over the hot and humid summer months, so she was slightly out of practice. Fortunately, the wind was at her back, so she made good time. When she got close enough, she hopped into the water and flipped the kayak right-side-up. She searched the nearby waters, hoping against all hope to find some indication of life. But it was no use. The kayak had likely been drifting for some time. She couldn't even find the oar. She could only hope the driver had been wearing a life jacket and wasn't at the bottom of the gulf.

As Connie hopped back on her board, the sound of sirens blared in the distance. Connie turned back toward the shore and breathed a sigh of relief when she saw a uniformed police officer and Sapphire Beach Fire-Rescue rushing toward Andrea's body.

Connie paddled back to shore, this time more slowly. Zach and Josh arrived and took over crowd control just as she was paddling in.

A few minutes later, the medical examiner arrived. After the police had taken pictures and examined the corpse and the kayak, he took Andrea's body away.

At this point, the trauma of what happened seemed to be taking a toll on Stephanie. Her eyes filled with tears as she stared blankly into the distance.

Connie and Elyse brought her back to their lounge chairs and tried to comfort her.

"I'm so sorry this happened," Connie said, once they were all seated. "Would you like to tell us about Andrea?"

Stephanie wiped her tears with her beach towel. "Andrea first became my client a couple of years ago, and we just hit it off. We would go out to eat every so often to catch up on one another's lives. She was so full of life. A few weeks ago, Andrea injured her hip and became a client again." Stephanie smiled through her tears. "She teased me that she injured herself on purpose, because we hadn't seen each other in a while, and she wanted to hang out."

While they were talking, Josh came over, sat on the beach blanket and smiled warmly at Stephanie. "I'm sorry for your loss, Stephanie. Elyse said the deceased was a friend of yours."

"I texted Josh right after I hung up with the 9-1-1 operator and filled him in," Elyse said. "I figured he and Zach would want to get right over."

Stephanie nodded and repeated what she had just told Connie and Elyse. "When Andrea didn't show up for her physical therapy appointment this morning, I thought she just flaked. I called and texted her, then waited in her driveway for twenty minutes. I feel so guilty that I was actually *happy* she didn't show up."

"The autopsy will give us more information, but we won't have the results for a while. From what you know about her medical history, do you think she could have had a heart attack?" Josh asked.

"I'm obviously not a doctor, but Andrea was healthy and strong. She ate right, worked out regularly, and she recovered fast from her hip injury. Today would have been her last day of physical therapy."

Josh took notes as Stephanie spoke.

Stephanie leaned back in her chair and took a deep breath. "Do you have any idea what could have happened to her?"

Josh shook his head. "I'm sorry, but we won't know anything for a while. We're still interviewing bystanders, but so far nobody noticed anything unusual until the three of you discovered the body." Josh looked over at Zach and Sergeant Tim Donahue, who had arrived shortly after Josh and Zach. "I should get back to helping with the interviews. Judging from their expressions, they aren't having much success, either."

"I just can't believe it," Stephanie said after Josh left. "How could this have happened?"

"Tell us more about her," Connie said, hoping to help her friend process her loss.

"Andrea moved to Sapphire Beach ten years ago to escape the cold Chicago winters. She loved her job as the executive assistant to the president of *Harold's Furniture*."

Josh and I bought our bedroom set at their Fort Myers store," Elyse interjected. "Isn't that a chain furniture company?"

"Yes," Stephanie said. "They are headquartered in Fort Myers, but they have stores throughout the country. Having had a similar job at the Chicago store, Andrea always said the company felt like a home away from home. She wanted to move to a warmer climate, so when the position opened in the Fort Myers store, she jumped at the opportunity."

"So, she spent most of her time working and enjoying an active, outdoor lifestyle," Connie said.

Stephanie nodded. "She also enjoyed volunteering on Saturdays at the Sapphire Beach Historical Museum. She had a passion for local history."

"What happened to her hip?" Connie asked.

"According to Andrea, she was a klutz. She recently purchased a recliner, and apparently she sat in it too hard and it flipped over."

"That's hilarious," Connie said. "Sounds like she really *was* a klutz."

Stephanie chuckled. "She kind of was. She was one of those people who was extremely athletic and coordinated, but she would trip walking off the dance floor. She used to make me laugh. But this time, there might have been more to it."

"What do you mean?" Connie asked.

"I examined the recliner that flipped over, and it was cheaply made. I don't think Andrea's injury was a result of clumsiness. Since she bought the recliner at *Harold's Furniture*, I insisted that she talk to her boss about examining their stock and potentially discontinuing the product if it was a widespread problem."

"Isn't it strange that Andrea would go kayaking just before a physical therapy session?" Elyse wondered aloud. "I would think she would want to conserve her strength for her therapy."

Stephanie shook her head. "Not really. As I said, this was her last session, and she was mostly healed. She was in excellent physical shape, so she recovered quickly. She was one of those rare clients who would do every exercise I gave her as often as I instructed her. She was just going for a light paddle. I told her I thought she should be fine, but to stay close to the shore and to head in if her hip started to bother her."

"Well, something went desperately wrong on that kayaking expedition," Connie said. "Assuming that Andrea didn't die of natural causes, can you remember anything from your conversations with her that might give us a clue about what happened to her?"

Stephanie bent her knees and hugged her legs as she considered Connie's question. "I really can't think of anything. I know she was on vacation from work this week, and she said she planned to kayak as much as possible now that the weather was cooling off."

Stephanie furrowed her brow.

"What is it?" Connie asked.

"Connie, do you really think there was foul play involved with Andrea's death?"

Connie shrugged. "It could have been an undetected heart condition or another issue such as an aneurysm. Even young and healthy people die unexpectedly. But what bothers me the most is the other kayak. If Andrea had a heart attack, who was the other kayaker, and where is he or she now?"

"Or more likely, where is his or her *body*?" Elyse asked.

Stephanie's eyes flew wide open.

"What is it?" Connie asked.

"I just remembered something. As I told you, when I scheduled Andrea's appointment for today, I asked her if we could make it earlier in the morning because of our beach day. She said she couldn't

22

make it before 11:00, because she needed to make a quick stop by the office first thing in the morning. Then she had a kayaking date at 9:00 with a guy she met online. With the shock of finding her body, I completely forgot about our conversation."

"That must be who the other kayak belonged to," Connie said.

"It must be," Stephanie said. "I remember, because I commented to Andrea that most people get together for coffee or a drink when they meet someone online, but I had never heard of a kayaking date. Andrea said that if it didn't work out, at least it wouldn't be a total waste of a morning off. She'd still get to enjoy a paddle on the Gulf of Mexico."

Elyse laughed. "I guess when you look at it that way, it's kind of ingenious."

Stephanie smiled. "Andrea was very efficient. She didn't like to waste time or effort. That's probably what made her a good executive assistant."

"Do you know anything else about this guy she met online?" Connie asked.

"Over the past few weeks, she would give me occasional updates of their conversations during her physical therapy sessions. Let's see. They had been emailing for a while, then they had a few phone conversations. She was excited to meet him in person. I think she said his name was Jason, but she never mentioned a last name."

Josh had just finished interviewing a woman, so Elyse motioned for him to come over. "Steph, you should tell Josh about Jason."

After Stephanie filled Josh in, he excused himself and went to finish questioning potential witnesses.

"I wonder what happened to the online mystery man," Elyse said.

Connie crossed her arms. "I know. Was he some kind of psycho who killed Andrea, or did someone else kill them both?"

"He could have been an online predator," Stephanie said.

"If it was murder, since Andrea and Jason barely knew each other, it seems unlikely that someone would have a motive to kill them both," Elyse said.

"I agree," Connie said. "The question is, if it *was* murder, was it Andrea or Jason who was the killer's primary target?"

Chapter 3

BY 2:00, CONNIE WAS TIRED of sitting around and watching the police question potential witnesses. "Why don't we go upstairs to my condo? I'll make us some lemonade and we can relax on the balcony," she suggested to her friends.

Stephanie sighed. "Okay. I'm not much in the mood for a beach day anymore, anyway."

"At least we got a couple of quality hours in before everything went downhill," Elyse said. "I'll tell Josh that we'll be upstairs if he or Zach have any more questions for us."

Elyse returned within a couple of minutes. "We're all set. Let's get out of here."

The women shook the sand off their towels and packed up their beach gear. Connie loaded her paddleboard onto its carrier and pulled it back into her storage bin in the garage, while Elyse and Stephanie carried the cooler, chairs, and beach bags. Then they took the elevator up to the seventh floor, where Connie's condo was located.

Ginger, Connie's chestnut and white Cavalier King Charles Spaniel warmly greeted the women. Connie had inherited both Ginger and her gulf-front condo from her beloved aunt, Concetta Belmonte.

Connie bent down and scratched Ginger's head. "You are always a sight for sore eyes, sweet girl. I should probably bring you for a walk before we get lost in conversation."

"I'll take her for a walk while you get the refreshments," Elyse offered.

Connie gratefully agreed.

The women changed out of their bathing suits, and fifteen minutes later, they were relaxing on Connie's balcony, which overlooked the Gulf of Mexico, and enjoying a glass of Connie's famous lemonade. Her super-healthy concoction consisted of juiced watermelon and lemon. She even juiced some of the watermelon rind for added vitamins and chlorophyll. She had made a batch that morning in anticipation that she and her friends would likely end up at her place after their day on the beach. She just hadn't imagined it would be after discovering a body.

Connie also brought out some cheddar cheese and crackers and a small bowl of roasted cashews.

"I couldn't help but notice there's a letter on your coffee table addressed to Concetta," Elyse said, once they settled in.

"It came in this morning's mail. I'm not sure what to do with it, so I just left it there. There's no return address, and it feels invasive to read my aunt's mail, even though she is deceased."

"You should open it, especially since there's no return address," Elyse said. "Maybe it contains more information about how you can reach the sender. You wouldn't want anyone to think your aunt Concetta just ignored their correspondence."

"I know. I guess I'm just trying to work up the courage to open it."

"If you need any moral support, just let us know," Elyse said.

Stephanie nodded her agreement.

"Thanks."

Connie breathed in deeply. The breeze off the gulf was warm and her lungs felt cleansed from spending the day outdoors. If she closed her eyes, she could almost forget the image of the dead woman in the kayak.

Stephanie barely touched the snacks Connie had prepared, so Connie and Elyse polished off most of them.

"I can't believe this happened to Andrea," Stephanie finally said. "Who would hurt such a kind soul?"

"Despite how it appears, we still don't know for sure that she was killed," Elyse said.

"True," Stephanie said. "But if Andrea had a heart attack, then what happened to her date?"

"It certainly does appear as if foul play were involved," Connie said. "If Andrea simply got sick while they were kayaking, Jason would have called 9-1-1, or at least paddled to shore for help if he didn't have his phone."

"I suppose you're right," Elyse said. "Jason's kayak was overturned, and he was nowhere to be found. Those facts seem to indicate that he was either trying to make himself look innocent, or that he was as much a victim as Andrea. But it does seem to rule out that Andrea got sick."

Connie gazed onto the beach. Zach was still questioning witnesses, but Josh had left, presumably to talk with Andrea's friends. Forensic divers had arrived and were searching the waters, but Connie wondered how they could even know where to begin looking, since the kayaks had been drifting for so long.

The women came inside and sat with him in the living room.

"How's it going down there?" Connie asked.

"It could be better. The divers haven't found any sign of the second kayaker."

"Do you know where Andrea and Jason launched their kayaks?" Elyse asked.

"Josh went to speak with some of Andrea's friends and acquaintances, and they informed us that she usually parks her car at the public parking lot at the beginning of Sapphire Beach Boulevard and launches her kayak from the public beach. He took a drive by, and sure enough, her car was there. It was next to a car registered to a Jason White, so we're trying to track him down, as well. It seems likely that he's the same Jason who was with Andrea when she died. We're in the process of calling area hospitals, but it doesn't look good for Jason."

"Do you have any persons of interest yet?" Elyse asked.

"We're just beginning to investigate. It's not officially a murder investigation yet, but nonetheless we're interested in anyone who might have had a motive to harm her."

"I wish I could be more help," Stephanie said. "Andrea and I were friends, but we hadn't talked for months before she injured her hip. That was normal for us. We would lose touch for a while, then pick right back up where we left off."

Zach stood and smiled. "I'd better get back to it. I'll be in touch if we think of any questions you might be able to answer for us."

"I'll walk you to the elevator," Connie said.

Zach took her hand. "Thanks."

"I guess this means you're in for a busy week," Connie said as they waited for the elevator. "I hope you're still able to take some time off to spend with your parents."

"Josh is taking the lead on this one, but it will still be busier than anticipated. I'll just have to make it work."

"Then we're still on for dinner with your parents on Friday night?"

"Definitely." He kissed her as the elevator opened.

When Connie rejoined her friends in the living room, the smile from being with Zach still lingered on her face.

"It sounds like the police have a long road ahead of them with this case," Stephanie said.

"That's usually how it is with limited manpower," Elyse said.

All of a sudden, Stephanie shot up from the sofa. "I can't sit here any longer, or I'll go crazy. Do you suppose we could pay a visit to *Harold's Furniture*? Maybe someone there knows something about Andrea's mystery date. I got the impression the company was like a close-knit family."

"Josh would *not* be happy if he knew we were snooping around." Elyse said. "And what if the police are there? That's probably one of the first places they'll go."

"They'll never believe that we just happen to be shopping for furniture at Andrea's place of employment," Connie said.

"Can't we just take a drive over?" Stephanie asked. "If there's a police car in the parking lot, we won't go in."

"I suppose the rest of the day is shot, anyway," Elyse said. "And I don't have to pick up the girls for a couple of hours."

"Why not?" Connie asked. She brought the empty dishes and glasses, which were still on the balcony, back into the kitchen. Then they grabbed their purses and headed out.

They took Connie's silver Jetta to *Harold's Furniture*, which was a few towns over in Fort Myers. As they pulled into the parking lot, a police cruiser was exiting.

"It looks like we're in luck," Connie said. "The police are just leaving."

After they entered the store, the three women pretended to be browsing the furniture. They slowly walked past the couches, then they came to the recliners. Stephanie stopped short in front of a black leather chair.

"That's kind of cute," Elyse said. "Are you in the market for a recliner?"

"No." Stephanie gestured toward the chair. "That's the same type of recliner that Andrea injured her hip on."

"The one you told her to tell her boss to discontinue if he didn't want a lawsuit?" Connie asked. "Are you sure? A lot of these chairs look alike."

"Positive. I examined Andrea's closely after her injury. This is the one."

"If they are defective, why would *Harold's* still be selling them?" Elyse asked. "They must know what happened to Andrea."

"Now that I think about it," Stephanie said, "it was *Harold's* who was covering the cost of Andrea's physical therapy. They asked Andrea not to submit her claim to the insurance company."

"Are you saying that *Harold's* knew the recliner was dangerous and didn't want word getting out that it was defective?" Connie asked.

As they were talking, a young man whose name tag read "Jonathan," approached them. "Welcome to *Harold's Furniture,* ladies. This is a fantastic little recliner. You have good taste."

"We're just browsing." Connie decided not to mention Andrea's death, in case the eager young salesman didn't yet know what happened to his colleague. After all, it had only been a few hours since Andrea's body had been discovered. They had seen the police leave, but that didn't mean all the employees received the news. Instead, she tried a more indirect approach. "Actually, we're friends of Andrea Fontaine. She recommended we come in."

A young woman, presumably another salesperson, stood a short distance away. She was leaning forward, as if straining to hear their conversation.

Jonathan flashed them a friendly smile. "Oh, you're friends of Andrea's. She's on vacation this week, or I would take you to her office to say hello. She'll be back next Monday."

He clearly didn't yet know that Andrea wouldn't be back on Monday.

"Andrea is always raving about her boss," Stephanie said. "It must be Harold."

The young man chuckled. "I think you mean Calvin. He is the current president of the company. Harold was the original founder."

Stephanie blushed. "She never mentioned his name, so I just took a guess. She's always saying what a wonderful company it is to work for. Would we be able to stop in and say hello to Calvin? I feel like I know him through Andrea."

Jonathan motioned for the women to follow him. "I don't see why not. He's out back in his office. I'm sure he wouldn't mind if you said a quick hello." Jonathan walked them through the back of the store and down a connecting corridor leading to an office suite.

Connie heard footsteps behind her and turned around. The woman who seemed to be listening in on their conversation by the recliners was following them.

When Connie made eye contact with the young woman, she smiled politely and pointed to a door just ahead on the right. "Just going to the ladies' room."

Connie smiled and continued walking.

When they were almost at the end of the corridor, Jonathan gestured toward a large glass double door. "You should find him in there. I'd better get back on the floor."

Chapter 4

THE THREE WOMEN thanked Jonathan and entered the President's Suite through the large glass door. Just in front of the entrance was an L-shaped cherry wood desk with a bronze metal plate inscribed with Andrea's name.

Stephanie teared up when she saw the plate.

A few seconds later a man wearing a navy silk suit and greying hair around his temples, greeted them.

"Hello, ladies." He smiled and pointed toward the doors through which they had just entered. "The showroom is that way."

"We know," Stephanie said. "Jonathan brought us back here so we could say hello. You must be Calvin. I'm Stephanie, a friend of Andrea's. She always spoke so highly of you."

Calvin raised his eyebrows.

"We happened to be in the neighborhood and thought we'd stop in," Connie said. "Unfortunately, we were the ones who discovered her body. We saw the police leaving, so we assume you heard the news."

His expression softened, but Connie couldn't tell if it was forced or natural. "Yes. I was truly devastated to hear what happened to Andrea. She was one of a kind. How awful that you found her body."

"It was," Connie said, "We were on the beach when her kayak came drifting to shore."

"Andrea was a good person and a top-notch assistant. I don't know how I will ever replace her. She was a valued part of the *Harold's Furniture* Family."

"I was hoping you might be able to shed some light on what happened to my friend," Stephanie said. "Would it be okay if we asked you a few questions?"

He gestured toward a seating area behind a partition wall, which contained a chocolate brown leather sofa and two oversized armchairs. His demeanor was formal, and Connie felt like they were being ushered into a business meeting. But at least he was willing to talk.

Calvin held up his index finger. "Just give me one second. I'm starting a new prescription, and I'm due to take it now." They watched him through the glass wall as he entered an office, opened his desk drawer, popped a pill, and chased it with a sip of water.

While they waited, Connie picked up a framed family photo that was on the coffee table. It was a picture of Calvin, a woman who was presumably his wife, and two young men.

"You have a beautiful family," Connie said, when Calvin returned.

"Thank you."

The women sat on the sofa, and Calvin took one of the chairs.

"I doubt that I have any information that would help you. The last time I saw Andrea was on Friday, and, as I told the police, I didn't notice anything unusual about her behavior." Calvin smiled stiffly. "She was excited to have a week off. I asked her what her plans were, and she said she was taking a 'staycation.' She planned to kayak, lounge by the pool, and catch up on some reading. She deserved it. She worked hard."

"So, she didn't come to the office this morning?" Connie asked. "She mentioned to Stephanie that she planned to stop by."

"I don't think so. If she did, it was before I arrived. As I said, the last time I saw her was on Friday."

Stephanie swallowed hard. "Andrea wasn't alone when she died. She was on a kayaking date with a man named Jason, whom she met online. His kayak was turned upside down in the water, and his oar was missing."

"Yes, the police mentioned that."

"Did Andrea ever tell you anything about this man?" Connie asked. "Do you have any idea who he is?"

Calvin shook his head. "The police asked me the same question. She never mentioned her date. But then again, that's not unusual. Things have been so busy here the past few months that we didn't often have time to discuss our personal lives."

That made sense. Who talks about a first date with their boss? Connie thought.

"Thank you for taking the time to talk with us," Connie said. "We are truly sorry about your loss. I'm sure she will be hard to replace."

"That she will," Calvin said.

They were about to leave when Stephanie motioned for them to hold on. "I just have one more question. I wasn't only Andrea's friend, but I was also her physical therapist. I noticed that you still carry the recliner that Andrea was injured on. I was wondering if you plan to take it off the floor."

Calvin narrowed his eyes and stood up.

The women had no choice but to stand with him.

"The problem is not the line of recliners. It was simply the one Andrea happened to get. There must have been a problem with its assembly, because we haven't received any other complaints on that model, and we've sold dozens. We agreed to pay for Andrea's physical therapy, even though it really wasn't our fault. Now if you'll excuse me, I must get back to work."

He ushered them out, and before they knew it, they were standing in the hallway staring at one another. Calvin had disappeared into his office at the back of the suite.

"Well, we should be going now, Calvin. We'll see ourselves out," Elyse said sarcastically.

The same woman who had followed them into the hallway earlier exited the ladies' room, glanced at the three women, and slipped around the corner and back onto the showroom floor.

"That was a long visit to the ladies' room," Stephanie said. "We were talking to Calvin for at least ten minutes."

Connie nodded her agreement and started after her.

Stephanie and Elyse followed.

When they caught up with her in the sofa section, the woman pretended to be busy fluffing some accent pillows.

"Excuse me, ma'am," Elyse said. "We couldn't help but notice that you seemed to be following us. Did you know Andrea?"

Tears spilled from the woman's eyes. "I didn't mean to be intrusive, but I thought I overheard the police earlier saying that she died. I was just listening to see if it was true."

Connie put her arm around the woman's shoulders. "I'm sorry, but yes. It's true. We are the ones who found Andrea's body in her kayak on the beach earlier today. I'm Connie, and this is Stephanie and Elyse."

"My name is Shannon. Andrea and I didn't socialize a lot outside of work, but we always chatted and often ate lunch together. She was a lovely woman. At least she died doing what she loved."

"Shannon, we came into the store in hopes of learning more about Andrea's final moments," Connie said. "She had a first date this morning with a guy named Jason, whom she met online. It was a kayaking date. Do you know anything about him?"

"You mean she wasn't alone when she died? Did the man try to get help when she fell sick?" Shannon asked.

"I wish we knew," Connie said. "There was a second kayak not far from Andrea's. We assume it belonged to Jason. The second kayak was overturned, and there was no oar anywhere in site. The kayaker hasn't yet been located."

"Oh, no," Shannon said. "Do you think there was foul play involved in her death? I hope she didn't have a date with a dangerous man."

"That still remains to be seen," Connie said. "Are you sure Andrea never talked about him with you? Any information would be helpful."

Shannon appeared to be searching her mind. "No," she finally said. "I don't think she ever mentioned a Jason, and she definitely didn't tell me about a date with someone she met online. I mean, we weren't extremely close."

Stephanie's shoulders slumped in disappointment.

"But I might know someone who can help you. Andrea's best friend was Cassie Beaumont. They volunteered together at the Sapphire Beach Historical Museum. Occasionally, she would stop by the office, and she and Andrea would go out to lunch. I'll bet she'd be able to answer any questions you may have about Andrea."

"You don't by chance know how we could reach Cassie, do you?" Stephanie asked.

"Unfortunately, I don't have her contact information, but I know she lives in Sapphire Beach."

They thanked Shannon for her help and returned to the car.

"Since Cassie is right in Sapphire Beach, we could do an online search to try to find her address," Connie suggested as she started the engine. "How many Cassie Beaumonts could there be in Sapphire Beach?"

"Already done," Stephanie said, holding up her phone. "There is only one. She is forty-three years old and lives at 17 Cypress Lane."

"That's only a few miles from Palm Paradise," Elyse said. "We practically have to pass that street to get back to Connie's. Let's plug it into the GPS and spin by."

Just as the words came out of Elyse's mouth, Stephanie's phone announced, "Directions to 17 Cypress Lane."

"I'm already on it," Stephanie said, laughing.

"It's not 5:00 yet," Connie said. "She might still be at work."

"Are you telling me that if you found out that Stephanie or I just died, you wouldn't even take the rest of the day off work?" Elyse asked, pretending to be highly insulted.

Connie laughed. "I guess you're right. If her best friend just died, she's probably at home. Let's go and offer our condolences."

"I wish we had a casserole to bring," Stephanie said.

Connie and Elyse agreed, so they did the next best thing they could think of in a pinch. They stopped at Publix and picked up a tray of cold cuts and a large bag of rolls.

"This will have to do on short notice," Stephanie said, as she placed the tray and rolls in the trunk.

They drove a few miles down Sapphire Beach Boulevard until they reached Cypress Lane, and Connie parked her Jetta on the street in front of number seventeen. Stephanie took the cold cut platter out of the trunk and Elyse took the bag of rolls.

They walked down a short path to the front door, and Connie rang the doorbell.

Chapter 5

A FEW SECONDS LATER, a woman with narrow blue eyes and short, light brown hair greeted Connie, Stephanie, and Elyse. There were dark circles beneath her bloodshot eyes, and she clenched a white tissue. The woman looked down at the platter of cold cuts that Stephanie was holding, then back up at the three women. She appeared to be searching their faces, feeling as if she should know them.

Seeing that the woman was uncomfortable, Connie said, "Hi, are you Cassie?"

"Yes, I am. How can I help you?"

Stephanie handed Cassie the cold cut platter. "My name is Stephanie, and these are my friends,

Connie and Elyse. I knew Andrea. We came to offer our condolences."

Cassie smiled. "Thank you. That's very kind. Please, won't you come in."

Elyse gently placed the bag of rolls she was carrying on top of the cold cut platter, and they followed Cassie to the living room.

"This is very thoughtful," Cassie said. "I'm not in the mood to cook, and I was getting hungry. Please, sit down."

The women sat on Cassie's couch.

"It was nice of you to stop by. I remember Andrea talking about you, Stephanie. You were also her physical therapist, weren't you?"

"I was. When I helped her with an injury a few years ago, we became friends. She started coming to me again about a month ago for another injury."

"Ah, yes, the rolling recliner." Cassie went into the kitchen. Her home was open-concept, so Cassie was still in view as she put the platter in the refrigerator and pulled out a pitcher. "Would you like some iced tea?" she asked. As if on autopilot, Cassie began filling four glasses before the women could answer.

"Thank you," Elyse said.

Stephanie hopped up and went into the kitchen to help Cassie carry the four glasses.

"It's nice of you to come by," Cassie said. "I was at work today when I received the news. I took the rest of the afternoon off, and I've just been moping around here ever since. How did you know my address?"

"Shannon, from *Harold's Furniture*, told us that you were Andrea's best friend and that you lived in Sapphire Beach, so we looked it up," Connie said. "I hope you don't mind."

"Of course not. I appreciate the company."

After Cassie recounted several stories of adventures she had shared with Andrea over the years, Connie moved the conversation toward Andrea's death. "The three of us were the ones who found Andrea's body this afternoon. We were hoping to learn more about what happened. Would it be okay if we asked you some questions?"

"I suppose," Cassie said. "But I talked to the police earlier, and I'm afraid I wasn't very helpful."

"Then they probably told you about the second kayak that was found upside down near Andrea's," Elyse said.

"They did. They don't know if Jason is alive or dead."

"Did you know Jason?" Stephanie asked.

"Not personally. I didn't even know his last name until the police told me. I only knew that Andrea met a man online named Jason. After getting to know each other through a dating app, they decided to meet in person. Andrea suggested they make it a kayaking date." Cassie smiled. "She said if the guy didn't like to kayak, the relationship would never work, anyway. She was thrilled to learn that he had his own kayak, and they made a date for Monday morning. I remember teasing her and saying that if he was free on a Monday morning, it probably meant he didn't have a job. But she said he was self-employed and was able to juggle his schedule. Andrea said she made a physical therapy appointment at 11:00, so that if the date wasn't going well, she wouldn't have to endure it for too long."

"She never showed up for her appointment," Stephanie said. "I called and texted her, but I obviously didn't hear back. Now I know why."

"I'll never forgive myself if Jason hurt her. I should have insisted she meet him for the first time in a public place. The Gulf of Mexico obviously wasn't public enough," Cassie said.

"It's always possible that she died of natural causes," Stephanie said.

"Or there could be another answer," Elyse added. "We are just asking around a little. Connie is a gifted amateur sleuth."

"Well, I appreciate anything you can do to help the police," Cassie said.

"I know it might be hard to think about, but do you know of anyone who might have had a motive to hurt Andrea?" Connie asked.

Cassie folded her arms, as if trying to protect herself from the thought of anyone hurting her friend, and she leaned back in her chair. "Andrea was not the type of person who you would think would have a lot of enemies. She was an introvert who spent her free time enjoying the southwest Florida climate and volunteering at the museum.

She had a few friends, but other than that, she mainly kept to herself. She was a homebody when she wasn't enjoying the outdoors."

"Did she have any enemies at all?" Connie asked.

Cassie let out a sigh. "There are a couple of situations in Andrea's life that could potentially have turned dangerous."

"In addition to her date with Jason?" Stephanie asked.

"Yes," Cassie said. "A few Saturdays ago, at the museum, we received a special donation. It was a beautiful hand-carved desk from the late nineteenth century. The piece had been in the Cartwright family for more than a hundred years."

"Who's the Cartwright family?" Connie asked.

"They were one of the first families to settle in what is now Sapphire Beach," Elyse said.

"That's right," Cassie said. "We were thrilled to receive the donation. We all admired it, volunteers and staff alike. The following Saturday, when Andrea and I went back to volunteer, we decided to take another look at the desk. Andrea said she had done some research and told me about a secret compartment, which that design often contained. It turned out Andrea was right. She found the compartment, and when she opened it, she discovered an old letter dating back to 1995. The letter contained some pretty telling information, which the Cartwright family didn't want to become public."

"What did the letter say?" Connie asked.

Cassie hesitated. "I really shouldn't say. It contained extremely private information."

"You can trust us," Stephanie said. "Whatever you tell us will not go any further than this room. We're not interested in gossip. We just want to know what happened to Andrea."

Cassie scrutinized the women. "If you promise. I could get into big trouble at the museum."

"We promise," Connie said.

"It was a deathbed letter from a Margaret Cartwright to her son, Henry, telling him that his biological father was not Margaret's husband, George, but the gardener. It went on to say that while George was off fighting in World War II, Margaret had had an affair that resulted in a pregnancy. The affair happened shortly after George left for the war, so he logically assumed that he was

Henry's father. As you can imagine, if word of this got out, it could cause the family a lot of unnecessary embarrassment. It would mean that Henry and his heirs are not technically Cartwrights."

"Did you return the letter to the family?" Connie asked.

Cassie shook her head. "Shortly after making the donation, the family realized their mistake. Henry's grandson, a guy named Nate, asked for the letter back. Andrea didn't feel as though she had the authority to return it to the family since the museum's curator, Michelle, was on vacation. Andrea stored the letter in a file cabinet for safe keeping and was planning to pay Michelle a visit this afternoon, after her physical therapy appointment, to tell her about the letter. But she obviously never made it. The letter is still in the museum. I'll talk to Michelle when I'm feeling up to it to fill her in."

"Wow, that's quite a story," Stephanie said.

"How did Nate react when Andrea told him she was going to turn over the letter to the curator?" Connie asked.

"He was pretty angry. He insisted the letter belonged to his family and that she had no right to hang on to it, but since Nate didn't know where the letter was, he had no choice but to leave. He didn't want to make a scene for obvious reasons."

"You said there was someone else who might have had a motive to hurt Andrea," Connie said.

Cassie nodded. "His name is Jeremy. He works for *Harold's* as a furniture buyer. Last month we were at a Labor Day party at Jeremy's home. Every piece of furniture in his home was from the Concord Furniture brand."

"What's wrong with that?" Stephanie asked. "Maybe he likes the brand."

"It's the same brand that produced the recliner that injured Andrea."

"I'm not sure I follow you," Connie said.

"They're not a high-quality brand, so Andrea became suspicious. She wondered why a furniture buyer who knew his stuff would decorate his home with cheaply made furniture. So, she did a little investigating. It turns out that Jeremy was taking a kickback from the company for purchasing so much of their furniture. Andrea talked to the sales associates, and every one of them confirmed that

Jeremy told them to push Concord's pieces really hard."

Connie's eyes widened. "Did Jeremy know about the recliner malfunctioning?"

"He must have. I think that's why they didn't remove them from the floor. Jeremy had purchased too many of them, and he didn't want to lose them as a customer because of his kickback."

"Do you think Calvin knew about that?" Connie asked.

"I can't say. He usually does whatever Jeremy says. They go way back."

The women thanked Andrea for the information and exchanged phone numbers, promising to keep Cassie posted on anything they learned.

Chapter 6

WHEN THE WOMEN returned to Palm Paradise, Stephanie and Elyse went back to Connie's condo to get their beach bags.

As Stephanie threw her pink and grey bag over her shoulders, she sighed. "I imagined we'd be returning to the condo after a day on the beach about this time. I had no idea we'd be returning from investigating the suspicious death of a friend."

"It's been a long day," Connie said. "Why don't you stay for supper? I don't have much in the fridge, but we could send out for pizza and take it easy tonight."

"I appreciate the offer, but I think I'll just go home and wind down. I have a long day at work tomorrow. I scheduled some of today's clients for tomorrow so I could take most of today off. As far as days off go, this one was a bust."

"I'd better leave now, too, or I'll be late picking up the girls," Elyse said.

Connie scooped up Ginger, who wasn't used to being alone all day, since Connie normally took her into the shop. "I guess my best girl and I will enjoy a rare evening at home. Tomorrow is Tuesday, which means I'm alone in the store all day, so I guess it will be good to call it an early night."

After her friends left, Connie took Ginger for a long walk along the beach. The dog was due for a bath, so it wouldn't do any harm if she got all sandy. Instead of taking a right on the beach and walking in the direction of the pier and downtown, Connie was drawn to go in the other direction. Probably because that was where the kayaks floated in from that afternoon.

Connie gazed down the beach as she walked along the hard sand. There was a long stretch of residences followed by a public beach, where Andrea and Jason had launched their kayaks from this morning. Zach had said that nobody on the beach saw anything helpful. They must have paddled out a fair distance for nobody to have noticed anything suspicious.

Connie allowed the waves to crash on her feet, hoping the rhythmic tide might help calm her thoughts. She wasn't just preoccupied with Andrea's death. She was also nervous about meeting Zach's parents on Friday. If she were honest, she was more than nervous. She was kind of terrified. What if it didn't go well? Elyse had met them before, and she assured Connie that they were great people. Elyse was a good judge of character, so that was comforting. "Well, Ginger," she said softly, "if they raised a son as amazing as Zach, they have to be pretty special."

When Connie got back upstairs, she gave Ginger a bath and heated up some not-so-exciting leftovers. Then she spent the remainder of the evening relaxing on her balcony with a mystery novel and a glass of chardonnay.

The following day was uneventful. Connie was alone at *Just Jewelry*, so she spread out her jewelry-making supplies on the oak table, and in between serving customers, she created several pairs of beaded dangle earrings in lavender, aqua blue, yellow, and black.

Some of the snowbirds had already returned from their summers up north, but the real onslaught would begin in January. Now was the time for Connie to be sure her inventory was well stocked for the busiest months, when customers would abound and there wouldn't be much time to create jewelry.

About 4:00, Elyse unexpectedly stopped by carrying a biodegradable cup carrier containing three coffees. She sat across from Connie and handed her one of the coffees.

"Thanks. You're a lifesaver," Connie said, savoring her first sip. "My energy level was just starting to drop. Who is the other coffee for?"

"Stephanie. She just texted me. She's finishing up with a client down the street and asked if we could meet here. I think she wants to talk about Andrea."

A few minutes later, a tired-looking Stephanie came in and plopped down in the chair next to Elyse.

"Long day?" Elyse asked, handing her a coffee.

Stephanie leaned back in the chair. "Yeah. And I didn't sleep a wink last night thinking about Andrea.

I wish I could erase the image from my head of the kayak drifting to shore with her body inside."

Connie gave Stephanie a hug. "That must have been quite a shock to realize that not only was there a dead body in the kayak, but that it was someone you knew."

Connie pushed her jewelry-making supplies to the side. "I've been thinking about it, too, especially after our conversations yesterday with Calvin, Shannon and Cassie."

"So have I," Elyse said.

While they were talking, Zach came into the store. He had been spontaneously stopping by more than ever in the past several months, and Connie was always glad to see him.

"Hi ladies. I didn't know you were having a party. My invitation must have been lost in the mail."

"It was just a last minute get-together," Connie said. "I didn't even know I was hosting a party until Elyse showed up with three coffees."

"I would have made it four if I knew you were coming," Elyse said.

"I just came by to say hello," Zach said with a smile. "I was in the neighborhood."

He was leaning in to kiss Connie when his cell phone rang. Startled, they both pulled back and laughed. Zach glanced at the screen. "It's Josh. I'm still on duty, so I'd better take it," he said, stepping to the other side of the store.

"So much for visiting," Zach said as soon as he disconnected the call. "They located Jason White, the man who was in the second kayak."

"You mean Jason's alive?" Connie asked.

"He's at a hospital in Fort Myers. Josh and I are going over now to see what happened." He smiled at Connie. "I'll try to come by later."

"Well, that's interesting," Elyse said after Zach left. "If Jason is in the hospital with injuries, then he likely isn't the killer."

"I wanted to get the three of us together this afternoon to discuss our next move, but this changes everything," Stephanie said. "We can't do anything until we hear what Jason's story is."

"Zach said he was going to try to come back later. I'll see if I can get any information out of him tonight," Connie said. "I'll be in touch later on."

"I'll try to get Josh to talk, too, but it's unlikely," Elyse said. "He's pretty tight-lipped about his cases."

Tuesday evening flew by in a haze. It was even busier than the afternoon had been. Connie was thrilled to sell one of her most expensive necklaces. Last summer she had planned to hire extra help for the busy season, but now that she had purchased the building that housed her shop and had a mortgage on her shoulders, she was hesitant to take on extra payroll expenses. However, if her most expensive pieces continued to fly off the shelf, she might be able to start looking.

Shortly before it was time to close the store, Zach returned.

"Party over?" he asked.

"Yeah, it broke up just after you left."

Since the streets were emptying out and it didn't look like there would be any more customers, they sat in the seating area. Connie relaxed on the red sofa, where she could keep an eye on the door - just in case - and Zach sat facing her in an armchair.

She was too curious about his conversation with Jason to make small talk, so she got right to the point. "Were you able to talk with Jason White?"

"Josh and I finished talking with him about an hour ago. He is being released first thing in the morning. Since he lives alone, the doctors decided to admit him for observation yesterday and today, but they are confident he'll be okay. He was more traumatized by the ordeal than anything else."

"Did he tell you what happened?"

Zach hesitated. "Well, I suppose it's not a secret. It will probably be in the news, anyway, in the next couple of days. Jason confirmed that he had a first date with Andrea yesterday morning. When they first met in the parking lot, she complained of a stomachache and fatigue but insisted she felt well enough to kayak. Jason didn't think much of it, because he thought she was just making it up so that she'd have an excuse in case the date didn't go well."

Connie chuckled. "That's the oldest trick in the book."

Zach smiled wryly. "I'm glad you didn't do that on our first date. Anyway, Jason said he feels terrible that he made that assumption. He said that if he had believed she was truly ill, he might have suggested they go for coffee instead, and she might still be alive."

"He shouldn't be so hard on himself. He couldn't have known."

"That's what we told him. Even though it was just a short date, Jason went all out. He brought some chocolate-covered strawberries and sparkling water to make it special, which they enjoyed once they were out on the gulf. A few minutes after they finished eating, she collapsed in her kayak and passed out. Jason had some rope, so he fastened their kayaks together and started to tow her to shore. He was so shaken up that he didn't see a speedboat approaching until it was right behind him. At first, he thought its driver was coming to help them, but then he saw that the man was wearing a ski mask that covered his entire face. While he was processing the scene, the man grabbed Jason's oar, whacked him off the head, and flipped over his kayak before speeding away. Jason couldn't even identify the boat. He only remembered that it was white, but that obviously doesn't narrow it down very much."

"How did Jason survive if he was unconscious in the water?"

"Fortunately, he had a life jacket on. He came to shortly after. He said Andrea was still breathing at that point, but the driver had taken Andrea's oar, as well. He had no choice but to swim to shore as fast as he could. He ended up quite a distance away from the public beach, where they originally launched their kayaks from. He landed on private property, but he passed out again. By the time anyone found him, a couple of hours had passed. He didn't have any ID on him. As soon as he woke up, he told the doctor his story."

"Wow, what a horrible ordeal," Connie said. "Unless, of course, he killed Andrea and fabricated the whole story."

"That would have been difficult. He was pretty traumatized, and there's no way he could have self-inflicted a wound on the back of his head to create an alibi. Besides, he had no reason to hurt Andrea."

"That means someone was definitely trying to kill Andrea, and not Jason. The speedboat driver had every opportunity to kill Jason if he had wanted."

"It looks that way. Jason simply got in the way of their plans to kill Andrea."

"So, the killer must have poisoned Andrea at some point that morning and followed her to make sure she died," Connie said.

"That's a strong possibility. We'll know more when we receive the toxicology report, but at this point, it doesn't look like Andrea died of natural causes. Otherwise, the speedboat driver wouldn't have knocked out Jason to ensure that Andrea didn't get the help she needed."

"When the killer saw that Jason was going for help, he probably panicked and hit Jason to ensure that Andrea wouldn't make it."

Zach nodded.

"Is there any way of tracking down that boat?"

"Unfortunately, Jason didn't get a good look at it, and it could have come from anywhere. He didn't see the person who hit him. He couldn't even verify whether it was a man or a woman."

"Poor Jason," Connie said. "It couldn't have been the sparkling water and strawberries that they ate, because Jason didn't get sick."

"That's right. Jason said that Andrea didn't have much of an appetite. He ate a lot more than she did. It had to be something Andrea consumed earlier.

When we found her car, we also discovered a travel mug filled with coffee in the cup holder, so we're having that analyzed. Stephanie said that Andrea had been planning to run a few errands before her date, so we're trying to retrace her steps that morning."

Chapter 7

CONNIE TRIED TO KEEP herself occupied for the remainder of the evening, but her mind kept drifting back to Andrea and her final moments of life. After closing the shop, she took Ginger for a walk then headed home for the night. She fixed herself a snack and a cup of herbal tea, then texted Stephanie and Elyse and summarized her conversation with Zach.

Stephanie was the first to text back. *That changes everything. Now we know two things: Jason was an innocent bystander and somebody targeted Andrea specifically.*

Elyse chimed in. *Talk about the worst first date ever!*

After we talked this afternoon, I remembered something, Stephanie said. *On Monday mornings,*

Andrea had a cleaning lady who came to her house. I remember because whenever Andrea would have physical therapy on a Monday, we'd have to go to the spare bedroom to stay out of her way.

That's interesting, Connie said. *If the cleaning lady was at her house yesterday morning, she would have had access to Andrea's coffee. She could have poisoned her.*

The woman's name was Cathy but that's all I know, Stephanie said.

I wonder if Cassie would know her last name, Elyse said.

Maybe. I'll call her tomorrow and find out, Stephanie said.

Perfect, Connie said. *We'll look forward to hearing from you. Good night ladies.*

On Wednesday morning, when Connie arrived at *Just Jewelry*, Grace was already there. She rushed over to Connie and gave her a big hug.

"I'm so sorry that your girls' day at the beach ended so tragically. You three will have to plan another day to make up for this one. Abby and I will cover for you again."

"Thanks, Grace. That's sweet. But I feel worse for Stephanie. Andrea was her client and friend. Did you know her?"

Grace shook her head. "No. We never met, but Stephanie would talk about her sometimes."

Connie hid her purse behind the circular checkout counter in the middle of the store for safekeeping and filled Ginger's water bowl. When she went back out front, Grace was sitting at the table staring vacantly at the floor.

"Is something else bothering you, Grace? You look like you lost your best friend."

"It's just that... well... after watching you find Jacob Atkins' killer at Palm Paradise during the hurricane in August and hearing stories about all your sleuthing adventures, Stephanie is convinced that she can find Andrea's killer. I begged her to stay out of it, but she won't listen. Promise me you won't let my baby do anything foolish. I don't know what I would do if something happened to her."

Connie crossed her heart with her index finger. "I promise to keep an eye on her. We are communicating every step of the way. I won't let her get into trouble."

Out of the corner of her eye, Connie saw Gallagher crossing the street and holding two green smoothies. He came into the store and handed one to each of the women.

"Hey Gallagher, it's great to see you," Connie said. "Especially when you come bearing gifts."

He smiled and gave Grace a hug. Gallagher seemed to enjoy Grace's maternal attention as much as Grace loved to lavish it.

"This time, I have an ulterior motive," Gallagher said.

Connie smiled mischievously. "You mean besides earning brownie points with your girlfriend's mother?"

Gallagher laughed and put an arm around Grace's shoulder. "Is it working?"

Grace patted his arm. "Honey, you don't need to score any points with me. The smile my daughter has been wearing lately is more than enough for me."

"I actually came because Stephanie told me about what happened at the beach."

"Isn't it awful?" Grace asked. "My poor Stephanie."

"Connie," Gallagher said, "Stephanie seems convinced that her friend was murdered and is determined to find the killer. I know there's no talking her out of it, so I wanted to ask you if you'd keep an eye on her and make sure she stays out of trouble until the police solve the case."

Connie and Grace laughed, and Gallagher looked at them with his eyebrows raised.

"Grace just made me promise the exact same thing. Don't worry, we're just asking around for more information."

"I know firsthand how your innocent inquiries can turn into a full-fledged investigation. Remember what happened during the hurricane?" Gallagher had been Connie's sidekick during her previous murder investigation.

"And countless other times," Grace added.

Connie lifted her arms in surrender. "Okay, you two win. As I promised Grace, I won't let Stephanie put herself in any danger."

Gallagher hugged Connie. "You're the best. I'd better get back to work and help the staff get ready for the lunch rush."

Connie smiled broadly at Grace after Gallagher left. "Did you see how concerned he is for Stephanie? It's so sweet."

"It is. She lights up when she talks about him, too."

Around lunchtime, Connie's phone pinged with another group text from Stephanie to Connie and Elyse. *I called Cassie this morning, but work has been so busy that I haven't had a chance to text you. I filled her in on what we've learned so far. She said the cleaning lady's name is Cathy Reardon and Cassie said she cleans Andrea's house at 8:00 every Monday morning. Andrea's place isn't very big, and she doesn't clean the guest room unless someone has been sleeping in it, so, by the time I arrived a little before 11:00 for Andrea's physical therapy session, Cathy could have been gone. That would explain why she didn't answer the door when I knocked.*

That means that Cathy would have been one of the last people to see Andrea alive, Elyse said.

We need to learn more about her and try to find out if she had a motive, Stephanie said.

Connie went to her computer and did a search for "Cathy Reardon cleaning services Sapphire Beach," but nothing came up.

Connie texted the group. *She doesn't have a website. It must be a small cleaning business.*

Maybe she only has a few clients, Elyse said. *She could work mothers' hours and rely on word of mouth for advertising.*

I found her address, Stephanie said. *There's only one Cathy Reardon in Sapphire Beach. We could pay her a visit and try to get some questions answered.*

Grace is leaving soon, then I'll be alone in the store until closing. How about tomorrow?

I could break away between clients about 10:30, Stephanie said.

Works for me, Connie said. *Grace will be here.*

Works for me too, Elyse said. *I'm not showing any properties until the afternoon. Let's meet in the parking lot of Palm Paradise.*

The rest of Connie's day was relatively uneventful. She created a few more pairs of earrings in between helping customers. After the long, slow summer season, it was nice to see business picking up again.

On Thursday morning at 10:15, Connie left Ginger at the store with Grace and drove back to Palm Paradise to meet Stephanie and Elyse in hopes of catching Cathy Reardon at home.

"It's a long shot," Connie said, as she hopped into the backseat of Elyse's car. "If she has a cleaning business, she's likely not home."

Following Elyse's GPS, they pulled into an upscale neighborhood just a short distance away.

"I wouldn't expect a cleaning lady to live in a neighborhood like this," Elyse said.

"Maybe that's why she doesn't advertise her business," Connie said. "Maybe it's just a hobby."

Stephanie turned and looked incredulously at Connie. "Most people don't clean other peoples' houses for fun."

"I guess you're right. Look, the lights are on. Someone must be home."

"Are you sure you got the right address?" Elyse asked. "Maybe the Cathy Reardon that cleaned Andrea's house doesn't live in Sapphire Beach. Maybe she lives in another town."

"Anything is possible," Stephanie said. "Let's give it a try, anyway, since we're already here. I've met her before at Andrea's, so I'll know right away if she's the right person."

They walked along the travertine walkway to the large, wooden front doors to what they hoped was Cathy Reardon's house.

"This house is huge," Stephanie said. "How does she keep her clients' houses clean and still manage to stay on top of this one?"

"I once sold a home in this neighborhood for nearly one million dollars. And it looked about this size," Elyse said. "This can't be the same Cathy Reardon."

Connie rang the doorbell. "There's only one way to find out."

Chapter 8

ABOUT THIRTY SECONDS after Connie rang the doorbell, a woman who appeared to be in her late thirties answered the door. She wore sweatpants, and her dark hair was tied back in a ponytail.

"Good morning, Cathy," Stephanie said.

Cathy studied Stephanie's face, as if trying to place her.

"I'm Stephanie. We met a few times at Andrea Fontaine's house. I was her physical therapist."

"Oh, yes, of course. I thought Andrea had an appointment with you on Monday at 11:00. I was there cleaning until noon, but she never returned for the appointment. When nobody came, I figured she must have canceled it."

"I came for her appointment at 11:00 and rang the doorbell, but there was no answer," Stephanie said.

"I didn't hear the doorbell. You probably came when I was running the vacuum cleaner."

Cathy was either a good actress or had no idea that Andrea was dead. Hadn't she seen it on the news?

"It sounds like you didn't hear the unfortunate news about Andrea," Connie said.

"I'm sorry," Stephanie interrupted. "I didn't mean to be rude. These are my friends, Connie and Elyse."

"Nice to meet you," Cathy said. "What news are you referring to?"

"Andrea passed away on Monday morning while she was kayaking," Stephanie said.

Cathy's knees looked like they were buckling beneath her, so Connie placed a supportive arm beneath her elbow.

"How did it happen?" Cathy asked. "Did she drown?"

"No," Connie said. "The police haven't yet determined the cause of death, but they do suspect foul play."

"How awful. I can't imagine anyone wanting to hurt Andrea, but I suppose I didn't know her very well. Do they have any suspects?"

"They are still investigating. We are actually the ones who found the body," Elyse said.

"Wait. You all found Andrea's body?"

"Yes," Stephanie said. "We were at the beach, and the kayak containing her body drifted to shore."

"That's horrible." Cathy paused as if trying to process the information.

Or trying to think of a way to cover her tracks.

"I saw her on Monday morning while I was cleaning her house. She had plans to go kayaking with a gentleman she met online." Cathy's eyes widened. "Do you think *he* killed her?"

Stephanie shook her head. "The police have ruled him out as a suspect. It seems he was just as much of a victim as Andrea. He is lucky to be alive."

The women were still standing in Cathy's entryway.

"Since you were one of the last people to see Andrea alive," Connie said, "we were hoping we could talk to you for a few minutes."

"I really don't know anything," Cathy said. "I need to process all this. If you don't mind, I think I'd rather be alone."

Stephanie persisted. "It will only take a few minutes. We promise. We thought you could tell us what you remember about her final hours."

"I suppose. But just for a few minutes." Cathy motioned for the women to come inside and gestured for them to take a seat around the dining room table.

"So, you said Andrea was home when you arrived to clean her house on Monday morning," Connie said.

"Yes. I got there about 8:00, and Andrea was just about to leave. She said she was going to stop by the office. Then she came back about 8:45. She looked tired, so I helped her lift her kayak onto the roof of her car for her kayaking date. Then she drove away. That was the last time I saw her. She told me she'd be back at 11:00 for her physical therapy appointment. When she didn't return, I just assumed there was a change of plans. It never even crossed my mind that anything could have happened to her."

"Are you sure she went into the office?" Connie asked.

"Yes, I'm positive. It looked like something was bothering her when she returned, so I asked her if everything was okay. She told me she was having a disagreement with her boss, but she hoped that getting into the fresh air and sunshine would help her to forget about it."

Connie, Elyse, and Stephanie looked at one another.

Why did Calvin lie and say that Andrea didn't come by the office on Monday morning?

Connie looked directly at Cathy. "This part is important. Can you remember if she had her travel mug with her when she left to go to the office?"

Cathy nodded. "Yes, she had the travel mug when she left. She usually had a cup of coffee with her breakfast on the lanai, then she would take her second cup on the road. She must have been tired that morning, because she had brewed a larger-than-normal pot of coffee. She instructed me not to turn off the coffee maker, because she would be back for another cup later. When she returned from the office, she was still carrying the mug. She took it into the kitchen and filled it again. That's when I helped her load her kayak onto the roof of her car. As I said, she looked tired, which is why I offered to lend her a hand with the kayak."

"Thank you," Stephanie said. "One more question. I know you were only in her home once a week, and Andrea was usually at work while you cleaned her home, but did you ever notice anything that might lead you to believe that Andrea was in danger?"

"Of course not. But I usually just saw her in passing. She would be leaving for work as I arrived."

"Are you sure you don't remember any other details from Monday morning?" Connie asked.

Cathy thought for a moment. "Actually, there is one thing, but I doubt it's important. After she fastened her kayak to the roof, her neighbor, Tori, opened her front door and waved. Andrea went inside for a quick visit before leaving."

That was interesting. That's one more person who could have had access to Andrea's coffee mug – that is assuming the killer poisoned Andrea's coffee.

"Thank you," Connie said. "We appreciate your time."

As Cathy was walking them to the door, Elyse glanced around the house. "I hope you don't mind my asking, but from the looks of your home, it doesn't look like..." Elyse hesitated.

"It doesn't look like I need to be cleaning houses." Cathy smiled. "My husband recently took a job that meant a pay cut. I worked my way through college cleaning houses and offices, so I thought I'd take on a few clients to earn some extra money - just to take some of the pressure off my husband."

"I've been thinking about hiring someone to clean my condo every other week, but I haven't had a chance to research any cleaning companies," Connie said. "Are you taking on new clients?"

Her friends shot her a puzzled look, but Connie avoided their gazes. Since she had recently purchased her shop, her friends knew she was looking to cut expenses, not increase them. But fortunately, they didn't say anything.

"I live in a two-bedroom condo," Connie continued. "I'd love to get an estimate."

"I don't know," Cathy said. "I'm not really up for taking on any more clients. I was thinking of cutting back. Then, as an afterthought, she added, "Which condominium building do you live in?"

"Palm Paradise, right on the boulevard."

Cathy's eyes lit up. "Oh, yes, I know it well. I used to have a client in that building. It would be $150 to clean the whole condo." Cathy handed Connie a business card. "Call me if you'd like to set up an appointment."

"Thank you," Connie said, taking the card. "I will do that."

After the women got back in the car, Elyse asked Connie why she said she was looking for a cleaning lady.

"There's something about that woman that I just don't trust," Connie replied. "I wanted to keep the lines of communication open and have a reason to call her again if we need to."

"I know what you mean," Elyse said. "I suppose it's a plausible story, but I just don't buy it."

"We did learn a few valuable things, though," Stephanie said. "We now know that Andrea did stop by the office and that she had her travel mug with her from the time she left the house on Monday morning. Anyone with whom she came in contact from the time she left the house at 8:00 Monday morning to the time she met up with Jason could have poisoned her coffee, including Cathy. We also know that she went inside her neighbor's house. We need to figure out if she saw anyone else on Monday morning and who among them had a motive to kill her. That should narrow down our suspects."

Connie thought about what Stephanie said. "Unless, of course, Cathy lied to throw us off. Maybe she laced Andrea's coffee with a slow-acting poison and told us that Andrea took her travel mug with her to the office, so it would look like someone else had the opportunity to poison her."

"And she could have made up Andrea's disagreement with Calvin and the visit with her next door neighbor," Stephanie said.

"We don't even know for sure that Andrea was poisoned through her coffee," Elyse added.

"You're right," Connie said. "But it does seem like the most probable explanation. I hope the toxicology report and the test on the coffee comes back soon. If we knew what Andrea died of, and how fast-acting it was, that might give us some insight."

Elyse drove Connie and Stephanie back to Palm Paradise to retrieve their cars. As Connie was reaching for the handle to open the door, Elyse grabbed her arm.

"I have to tell you something. I've been wondering all morning if I should bring it up, but I'll just explode if I keep it to myself."

"Is it connected to the case?" Connie asked.

"No, it's nothing like that. This is *way* better." Her eyes sparkled with excitement. "I've been wondering if I should tell you or not, but I can't keep it in. Plus, I thought you'd want to know. I would if I were you."

Connie and Stephanie both burst out laughing.

"Elyse, you're not making any sense," Connie said. "What on earth are you talking about?"

Elyse smiled broadly. "Yesterday, I was driving to a showing in Naples, and I passed *Fiona's Fine Jewelry.*

"Oh, they have some beautiful pieces," Connie said. "They are top notch."

"I know. That's where Josh bought my engagement ring. Anyway, guess who was leaving the store with a small bag and a big smile on his face?"

Elyse looked at Connie, waiting for a reaction.

"Was it Zach?" Stephanie asked. "Do you think he was buying something for Connie?"

Elyse nodded. "It was Zach. And who else could it be for? Connie is his only girlfriend!"

Connie let go of the door handle and leaned back in her seat. "For one, he could have been buying a gift for his mother. His parents are coming to town, and it was her birthday a few weeks ago."

"True," Elyse said, appearing crestfallen. "I hadn't thought of that. But you should have seen his smile. It had to be for you."

"Are there any special anniversaries coming up for you and Zach?" Stephanie asked.

Connie shook her head "No. And it's too early for Christmas shopping."

"Let's just say for the sake of argument that it *was* an engagement ring."

"But..." Connie started.

Elyse held up her hand. "Just hypothetically. What would you say?"

Connie let out a deep breath. "I do love him."

Elyse let out a squeal. "I knew it. You'd say 'yes.'"

"There has been no indication that he's about to propose. Usually the guy at least drops some hints. Elyse, you're stressing me out! The more I think about it, I don't think I'm ready for marriage. I have too much going on."

"Well, you should think long and hard about what you would say. You two already act like an old married couple in a lot of ways," Elyse said.

"Elyse is right," Stephanie said. "You take care of each other like you were already married. You pretty much decorated his house, and he made sure your shop was up and running after the hurricane before he even took care of his own home. It's sweet."

For the rest of the day, Connie couldn't take her mind off Elyse's question. What would she say if Zach proposed? She had been through so much in the past few years. Did she really want another cataclysmic change in her life?

Chapter 9

ALL DAY ON FRIDAY, Connie's heart felt like it would beat through her chest. Despite Elyse's repeated assurances via text that she would get along just fine with Zach's parents, she was anxious about meeting them.

Even Grace tried to reassure her.

"I don't know why I'm so nervous," Connie said while Grace was eating lunch. Connie had taken a few bites of her sandwich, but then pushed it aside because she had no appetite.

"Of course you're nervous. You love Zach, and it's important to you that his parents like you."

"Yeah, I guess that's it." Connie decided not to mention Elyse's theory about Zach having purchased an engagement ring.

The afternoon dragged on, so Connie was thrilled when Abby arrived an hour early for her evening shift. "I knew you'd be nervous about tonight, so I thought you might want some extra time to get ready."

"You're the best!" Connie gave her a quick hug as she ran out the door, practically dragging Ginger behind her.

After walking Ginger, she showered and took her time getting ready for dinner at Zach's.

Zach picked Connie up right on time at 5:00 and brought her back to his house, where his parents were enjoying a pre-dinner glass of chardonnay on the patio. Zach's patio overlooked a canal, and the soft breeze, which floated in their direction, was refreshing.

When she saw their friendly faces, Connie felt a twinge of relief. Zach's father, Ben, had white curly hair, which was clean-cut, like his son's blond hair, and had clearly passed on his blue eyes to Zach. He was a little shorter and stockier than Zach's medium height and build. Zach's mother, Pauline, was a sturdy woman with friendly brown eyes. She was a ball of energy.

"So, this is the infamous Connie," Ben said, pulling her into a bear hug. "She's even prettier than you told us."

Zach smiled as he poured two more glasses of chardonnay and placed them on the table in front of two empty chairs.

"Zach told me that you recently celebrated a birthday, Mrs. Hughes, so I brought these for you." Connie handed Pauline a bouquet of sunflowers and a small gift bag.

Pauline hugged Connie. "The flowers are beautiful. And please, it's Pauline and Ben."

Pauline opened the box, revealing a black onyx bracelet Connie had made.

"I wasn't sure of your favorite colors, but I thought this would go well with a lot of different outfits."

"I told you she was talented," Zach said.

"I see you were right." Pauline slipped the bracelet onto her wrist. "It's lovely."

Connie sat at the table and sipped her wine. Her nerves had subsided at Pauline's and Ben's kindness, but she still felt a twinge of anxiety.

"Mom's been filling us in on some of the things she wants to do this week while she's in Sapphire Beach," Zach said.

Zach and his father exchanged an amused glance.

"Connie, I'm sixty-five years old this year, and I decided I need some adventure in my life," Pauline said. "As a wife, a mother of two boys, and a full-time nurse, I've always been cautious in my decisions. Now, I think it's my turn to live a little."

"That sounds like a good plan," Connie said.

Zach laughed. "Don't encourage her. I'm not going to be able to keep up with everything she wants to do *and* stay on top of a murder investigation at the same time."

"Okay, I'll pick a few things then. The most important one for sure is trying that boat thing we saw on the way from the airport. What was it called again, Zach?"

"A banana boat, Mom. You need a group for that."

"Well, we're a group right here," Pauline said, gesturing toward the four of them. "How about we make a day of it?"

"Mom, Connie is a business owner. I don't think she can take a whole morning off on such short notice."

"Don't worry about that," Connie said. "I could probably get Grace to cover for me on Wednesday morning. Pauline, would you like me to make the reservations? I've never done it myself, but it looks like loads of fun."

Pauline clasped her hands together. "That would be wonderful. Oh, I'm so excited. This is going to be a great vacation."

After they got acquainted and finished their wine, they got into Zach's Jeep and rode to the restaurant where he had made reservations. The hostess brought them to a table on the patio overlooking the water.

"Ah, this certainly beats the cold spell we've been having back home," Ben said. "There's nothing like a warm breeze coming off the water."

"Especially in late October," Pauline said. "The weather here is gorgeous."

"It is, as long as you avoid the hot summer months," Connie said. "But this time of year makes it all worth it. Have you ever considered moving to Sapphire Beach?"

"Our other son, Matthew, and his boys live the next town over from us back home, so it would be difficult to leave them." A mischievous expression spread across Pauline's face and she squeezed Connie's hand. "But who knows, maybe if our other son here gave us a reason, such as grandchildren, we'd consider purchasing a small condo in Sapphire Beach and spending the winter months here."

"Mom, I can't believe you actually said that out loud!" Zach said, shaking his head. His cheeks were redder than Connie had ever seen them. "You've barely known Connie for a couple of hours and you're bringing up grandchildren."

"Oh, Connie, don't mind us," Ben said. "It feels like we're old friends. Between all the wonderful things that Zach, Elyse, and Josh have told us about you over the past year-and-a-half, it feels like we've known you as long as they have."

"The feeling is mutual," Connie said, squeezing Pauline's hand in return.

Zach's cheeks hadn't yet returned to their normal color, so Connie resisted the urge to laugh at his discomfort. She didn't often see this shy-little-boy side of Zach.

After dinner and a leisurely dessert, Zach dropped off his parents at his house before driving Connie home. As Pauline was getting out of the car, she whispered to Connie, "I won't tell Zach that I love your bracelet more than the one he bought me." She pointed to a gold bracelet she was wearing along with the one Connie had given her. "You create the most exquisite jewelry."

"If you have a chance, stop by *Just Jewelry* sometime this week. I'd love to show you around."

While Zach walked his parents inside, Connie laughed and shook her head. After all Elyse put Connie through yesterday, Zach had indeed been buying a birthday gift for his mother when Elyse saw him leaving *Fiona's Fine Jewelry*.

When Connie and Zach returned to Palm Paradise, Zach accompanied Connie upstairs.

"I really enjoyed meeting your parents," Connie said. "I think they would get along really well with my parents."

"I think so, too. You'll like my brother Matt, as well. I hope he and his family are able to visit before too long." Zach chuckled. "I hope it won't be too difficult for you to get Wednesday morning off for the banana boat excursion. It's kind of out of character for my mother. Ever since she retired a couple of years ago, she's had this adventurous streak. My father, Matt, and I keep thinking it's just a phase, but then she surprises us again. My brother is going to crack up when he hears this one."

"I think it's great," Connie said. "She deserves to have a little fun in her retirement years. Besides, every time I see people on those boats bobbing up and down the coastline, it makes me want to try it."

Zach was about to leave, but he suddenly stopped. He picked up the unopened letter addressed to Concetta that was now on the dining room table. "What's this?"

"It came on Monday. It's addressed to my aunt, so it feels invasive to open it. But there's no return address."

Zach handed Connie the letter. "You should open it. It could be important."

A range of emotions flooded Connie's heart. As long as the letter remained unopened, it felt as though a part of Concetta was there. The letter held the promise of another conversation with her aunt. As she stared at the letter in her hand, Connie realized that, more than a fear of invading her aunt's privacy, that was the reason she couldn't bring herself to open it.

"I know. I will."

Zach sat at the table and motioned for Connie to do the same. "There's no time like the present," he said with a warm smile.

Connie took a deep breath. It would be comforting to open it while Zach was there for moral support. "I guess you're right." She slowly opened the handwritten letter and read it aloud.

My Dearest Concetta,

It certainly has been a while, hasn't it? I didn't include my return address on the envelope because I was afraid you might not open this letter if you knew it was from me. I'm asking you for the opportunity to finally clear the air between the two of us. I have carried what happened between us for more than forty years. I wouldn't blame you if you never wanted to talk to me again, but I am counting on you still having that same loving and forgiving heart that you had when we were teenagers.

On Sunday, November 1, I will be passing through Sapphire Beach. I hope that we can talk. Please meet me in the bar at Callaway's Restaurant at 1:30. I hope you will grant my wish.

Yours Truly,

Francis

"Wow, that's intense," Zach said. "Do you know who Francis is?"

Connie looked at Zach. "I have no idea. I never heard Aunt Concetta mention his name. I'll check with my mother. Maybe she knows."

"Are you going to meet him?"

Connie let out a quick breath. "I feel like I have to - for Aunt Concetta." Connie glanced at the letter in her hand. "And for this poor man. His words seemed to contain desperation."

"I suppose there's no risk, as long as you don't go anywhere with him. Stay at Callaway's and be careful." Zach leaned across the table and kissed her. "I'd better get back to my parents. Oh, and sorry about the grandkids comment. I can't believe my mother said that the very first time she met you!"

"Are you kidding? You met *my* mother! Those words could easily have come from her mouth. I had to reign her in big time when she first met you."

"I would have felt better knowing that beforehand." Zach smiled playfully at Connie. "But there's nothing wrong with our mothers wanting more grandchildren is there?"

Zach opened the door to leave without taking his gaze off Connie.

She returned his smile. "It sounds like a worthwhile desire to me."

His smile broadened as he closed the door between them.

After Zach left, Connie called her mother and read her the letter.

"That is so strange," Jo said. "I never heard Concetta mention anyone named Francis. It sounds like he might have been an old beau."

"I can't believe she never mentioned him to you, Mom."

"It's not really all that strange, honey. You have to remember, Concetta was five years older than me. When she left for Hollywood, she was eighteen, but I was only thirteen. Five years is nothing when you're an adult, but for teenagers, she might as well have been thirty. We didn't start sharing adult-type stuff until I was a little older."

"I guess that makes sense. I always forget that the two of you weren't as close in age as Gi and me."

"Are you going to meet this man?"

"I think I should. It's not until Sunday, so I have a couple of days to decide. But I think I've already made up my mind."

"Just promise you'll be careful and call me right after."

"I promise. I know the restaurant Francis suggested. It's right on Route 41 so there will be plenty of people around."

Chapter 10

ON SATURDAY MORNING, Connie woke up early to take Ginger for a long walk before work. As they were strolling along Sapphire Beach Boulevard, her phone, which was tucked in her pocket, rang. Not recognizing the number, Connie assumed it was a telemarketer. However, since she was in a good mood after her evening with Zach and his parents, she decided to answer it, anyway.

"Hello."

"Hi Connie, it's Cassie. I hope you don't mind my calling you so early."

"Not at all," Connie said. "I'm just walking my dog. Did Stephanie fill you in on what we discovered?"

"She did, and I'm calling to return the favor. I got a phone call early this morning from Michelle, the curator of the Sapphire Beach Historical Museum, where Andrea and I volunteered. Michelle said that someone broke into the museum."

"That's awful," Connie said, a little confused as to why Cassie felt the need to personally tell her about the theft. "Was anything valuable stolen?"

"At first, Michelle said nothing was missing. We thought it was strange that someone would break in and not take anything, but we figured maybe something scared them away before they had a chance to rob the place. I met her at the museum and looked around myself. At the last minute, we decided to search the offices, and sure enough, the letter that Andrea had found in the Cartwrights' desk was gone. Andrea had tucked it away in a drawer for safekeeping, until she was able to pass it along to Michelle, but, of course, she never had the opportunity. I was planning on doing it myself this week, but I've been sick the past few days and never made it over there."

"Are you sure someone didn't put the letter in another location?" Connie asked.

"I'm positive. Only Andrea and I knew where it was. It's definitely missing. I told Michelle the whole story. She was shocked and said that Andrea did the right thing in hanging onto the letter, but, ironically, Michelle said she would have been happy to return the letter to its rightful owner. If Nate or one of the other Cartwrights stole it, they wasted their time."

"I really hope Andrea wasn't killed over that letter," Connie said. "It would have been such a waste, especially since Michelle would have returned it, anyway."

"It had to be Nate who stole it," Cassie said. "Nobody else knew that we had the letter, except Nate and his family."

Connie reflected for a moment. "Actually, if Nate stole the letter, he probably didn't kill Andrea. He would have had no reason to kill her if he had been planning to break into the museum, anyway."

"I don't think that necessarily takes Nate off the suspect list," Cassie said. "As far as Nate was concerned, nobody knew about the letter besides Andrea. He didn't know she told me about it, and he didn't know that Michelle would have returned it to his family. If Andrea were still alive, she would suspect Nate of taking the letter, but with Andrea out of the way, as far as Nate knows, he's completely in the clear. Nobody has any clue about his family secret or that he would have any reason to break into the museum."

"That's a good point," Connie said. "We'll keep him on the list."

"That's not all," Cassie said. "I paid a visit to the staff at *Harold's Furniture* yesterday to thank everyone for their friendship towards Andrea over the years. She always said they were like a second family to her. I also took the opportunity to have a chat with Shannon to see if she noticed anything unusual around the store before Andrea's death. She wouldn't talk in the store, but it seemed like she had something she wanted to say, so I took her to lunch and I learned something interesting."

"About Calvin?" Connie asked.

"Calvin *and* Jeremy. Shannon was in the store on Monday morning, when Andrea came in."

So, Cathy was telling the truth about Andrea going to the office on Monday morning.

"Apparently, the reason Andrea went into work on a vacation day was to speak with both Calvin and

Jeremy about the recliner. According to Shannon, who was eavesdropping, Andrea told Calvin and Jeremy she believed that particular model was defective, and if Calvin didn't pull the chairs off the floor, she would be going public with the information."

"Does Calvin know that Jeremy is receiving a kickback every time he sells one of those recliners?" Connie asked.

"I don't know about that. But neither Calvin nor Jeremy wanted to discontinue the recliner, because they had so many of them in stock. They would have lost a *ton* of money. Shannon heard the three of them arguing about it, and the conversation ended with Andrea giving them an ultimatum."

"It seems our suspect list is growing," Connie said. "Cathy, Calvin, Jeremy, Nate, and Tori all either had a motive or the opportunity to kill Andrea. Now, we have to figure out who had both."

"Nate had the strongest motive, and he could have followed Andrea and found a way at some point that morning to slip something into her coffee."

"I agree," Connie said. "It sounds like we need to have another conversation with each of the suspects to see if we can glean any more information. But we'll have to think of a way to be discreet about it."

"One more thing, Connie. The recliners were still on the floor when I was in there yesterday."

After her conversation with Cassie, Connie took Ginger back upstairs and got ready for work. She left a few minutes early so she could stop by *Sapphire Beach Boat Rentals* to inquire about reserving a banana boat for Wednesday morning. She was looking forward to seeing Travis and Ashley, a young married couple from Boston who had relocated to Sapphire Beach. Travis was the first person to teach Connie how to paddleboard nearly two years ago.

When Ashley saw Connie and Ginger walking down the beach, she came out from behind the booth and hugged Connie. "Travis will be so sorry he missed you. He's working at the shop today." In addition to having a boat rental operation on the beach, they also had a store where they sold used equipment and organized excursions.

"Are you still loving life in Sapphire Beach?" Ashley asked.

"Absolutely. If I start to get homesick, all I need to do is take a walk on this beautiful beach and remember how cold it is back home right about now."

"Same with us," Ashley said. "I heard it's been unseasonably cold in New England."

"I came by to make a reservation for a group of four to do a banana boat ride."

"Are you one of those four?" Ashley asked, hopefully.

"Yes. It will be me, Zach, and his parents."

Ashley nudged Connie. "Ooh, meeting the 'rents for the first time?"

Connie laughed. "We met last night for the first time, and apparently Zach's mom, Pauline, has discovered her adventurous side since she retired."

Ashley let out a chuckle. "We specialize in adventure. When did you want to come?"

"How about Wednesday morning at 10:00?"

Ashley pulled out a lime green book and wrote down the reservation. "See you Wednesday at 10:00. You guys are going to have a blast."

Chapter 11

AFTER BOOKING THE RESERVATION for the banana boat ride, Connie and Ginger made their way to *Just Jewelry*. She texted Zach to let him know that she made the reservation, and also Grace, to give her a heads up that she wouldn't be in the store on Wednesday morning. Grace was probably on her way in, but Connie wanted to make sure she didn't forget to tell Grace about it.

They both replied with a thumbs-up emoji.

Grace arrived just a few minutes after Connie.

"Thanks for covering the store alone on Wednesday morning, Grace."

"Anytime, honey," she said. "I'm glad you're spending some time with Zach's parents while they're here. I'm sure it means a lot to them."

About 10:30, Connie received a text from Stephanie. *I just called Cassie to see how she was doing.*

I spoke with her a couple of hours ago, Connie replied.

She told me. She said her conversation with you gave her an idea. She has a spare key to Andrea's house and suggested we go over to see if we can find anything that might give us a clue about what happened. I know it's a long shot, but I told Cassie I'd ask if you thought it was a good idea. It would have to be today, though. Andrea's parents are flying in from Chicago tomorrow morning.

It couldn't hurt, Connie replied.

Connie looked up from her phone. "Grace, would you mind if I ran an errand?"

"Go right ahead."

Connie sent another text to Stephanie. *I can break away right now.*

I'll call Cassie to see if she is free.

And I'll text Elyse to see if she can come.

In less than a half hour, Stephanie had picked up Connie and Elyse, and they met Cassie in front of Andrea's house.

"Thank you for meeting me here," Cassie said. "I don't know if we'll find anything, but I need to try something." Cassie's eyes filled with tears as she unlocked Andrea's front door. "It's the first time I've been here since Andrea's death. I can't tell you how much I miss her."

Stephanie put a supportive hand on Cassie's shoulder as they entered.

Cassie pointed at a large beige sectional that surrounded a TV console with a built-in electric fireplace and a TV mounted on the wall above. "We spent so many nights watching movies on that couch."

Cassie took a deep breath. "I think this is a waste of time. I'm sorry I dragged you all out here. I'm not even sure what we should be looking for."

"Let's just walk through her home and see if we get any ideas," Connie said.

"Okay. But let's not disturb anything. When her parents come tomorrow to clean out her house, I want everything to be as she left it."

The women walked from room to room. There were a few papers piled neatly on the kitchen counter, which Connie perused, but she found nothing out of the ordinary - just some old bills and a bank statement. Her finances were in good shape, but nobody would be killing her for an inheritance.

It was evident by her home that Andrea had been an organized person. Everything seemed to be in its place, and, since Cathy had cleaned the house the morning of Andrea's death, everything was also sparkling clean.

The last place they searched was the study. A few more bills, but nothing unusual, as far as Connie could see.

While Connie was exploring, Cassie made a beeline for the desk chair in front of Andrea's computer. She picked up a white sweatshirt with the words "Sapphire Beach" written across the front in black. "This isn't Andrea's sweatshirt. I wonder who it could belong to?" She held it out in front of her and examined it more closely. "This is definitely too big for Andrea."

"You're right," Stephanie said. "Maybe it belongs to Cathy. She could have left it here when she was cleaning."

Connie inspected the sweatshirt. "I can't imagine anyone needing a sweatshirt this time of year during the day, but the evenings have been dropping into the sixties. Whoever left this probably came at night. I doubt it belongs to Cathy."

"You're right," Stephanie said. "Besides, Cathy probably works up a sweat cleaning the house. I doubt she wears a sweatshirt while she works."

"I'll hang on to it, anyway," Connie said. "It will give us another excuse to pay a visit to Cathy if we need to talk to her again."

Connie sat in Andrea's desk chair and booted up the computer. "That figures. It's password protected."

"I think I could figure out her password," Cassie said.

She made a few attempts, and just as Connie was having her doubts, Cassie received access. Cassie, Elyse, and Stephanie stood behind Connie as she opened Andrea's email inbox and scanned her unread messages.

"Nothing out of the ordinary so far," Connie said. After going through a few days' worth of messages, Connie leaned back in her chair. She was just about ready to give up when something occurred to her.

"Wait a minute. The most recent unread message is dated Tuesday morning."

Connie scanned Monday's messages. "And there are several messages that came in on Monday, the day Andrea died, that had already been read when we arrived."

"Maybe Andrea checked her messages on Monday morning," Stephanie said.

"But Andrea died on Monday morning, and some of these messages are from the afternoon and evening. Look, this last one came in at 7:07 PM. Somebody else was in her email account reading her messages on the night she died."

"Maybe it was a family member," Cassie suggested. "They could have checked her messages remotely. Even if they didn't know her password, they could have guessed."

"Or it could have been the police," Elyse said.

"I doubt that," Connie said. "The police were still busy questioning witnesses on Monday, and I don't think a family member would check her email the night she died and not go back to them for the rest of the week. I think it's more likely that someone was searching for something."

"But who?" Cassie asked. "And how? I think I'm the only one with a spare key to her house."

"What about Cathy?" Connie asked. "If she cleaned Andrea's house on Mondays when Andrea was normally working, she must have had a key."

"That's true," Stephanie said.

Connie looked through Andrea's messages - first her inbox, then her sent messages. When she got to the sent messages, she noticed an email from Andrea to Cathy Reardon. It read, "Cathy, we need to talk. Can you come a few minutes early on Monday morning?"

There was a reply from Cathy saying that she would be there at 7:45.

"That's strange," Elyse said. "Cathy didn't mention anything about that when we talked to her."

"Now we have two reasons to pay Cathy another visit - the sweatshirt and the email," Stephanie said. "We need to know what that message was all about."

"I still have some time before I have to be back at *Just Jewelry*," Connie said. "How about we stop by after we leave here?"

Everyone agreed, but Cassie decided she didn't want to go. "If Cathy doesn't have a solid explanation for that email, I don't think I could keep my cool."

While they were still there, Connie scanned the emails from the previous week, but nothing struck her as particularly suspicious.

"Let's go," Connie said. "I don't think we're going to find anything else here."

While they were walking back to the car, a short woman with red hair jogged toward them from the house next door. "Excuse me," she said as she got closer.

"Hi, Tori," Cassie said.

Tori stopped short before she reached the women and rubbed her right shoulder.

"Hi, Cassie. I saw you leaving Andrea's house, and I wanted to say how sorry I was to hear about what happened. I'm going to miss having Andrea as a neighbor."

"Thanks, Tori. I'm going to miss her, too."

"You look like you're in pain," Stephanie said. "Is your shoulder okay?"

"Yeah, I'll be okay. I must have slept wrong." Then Tori pointed to the sweatshirt Stephanie was carrying. "Hey, that's my sweatshirt. I was wondering where it went."

Stephanie handed Tori the sweatshirt.

"We found it by the computer in Andrea's office," Connie said. "Were you in there recently?"

Tori's eyes widened. "Um, yes. I was telling her about a new restaurant I had just tried, but couldn't remember the name, so we went into her office to look it up online. That's probably when I left it in there. Anyway, I just wanted you to know how sorry I am about Andrea. I was just getting ready for a waitressing shift, so I have to go."

"I thought you were a high school principal," Cassie said.

Tori looked at the ground. "I am, but I took on a second job for some extra money." Then she turned and left just as quickly as she arrived.

"That was bizarre," Elyse whispered.

Connie was afraid that Tori was still within earshot, so she put her index finger to her lips and motioned for everyone to get into Stephanie's car.

"I agree," Cassie said, once they had closed the doors. "It was bizarre. For one thing, she and Andrea were not exactly friends. They were friendly enough, but I highly doubt that she was at Andrea's house just hanging out."

"And I didn't buy her flimsy excuse about searching for a restaurant online," Elyse said. "They could have looked up the information on their phones."

Since Cassie had taken her own car to Andrea's, she exited Stephanie's car and got into her own. "Good luck with Cathy," she said as she was leaving. "Let me know how it goes."

As Stephanie was pulling away from Andrea's house, Elyse yawned. "Can we stop for a quick cup of coffee before we go to Cathy's? Victoria had a bad dream last night and woke us up at 3:00 in the morning, and I don't think I ever got back to sleep."

"There's a coffee shop on the way to Cathy's," Stephanie said. "We can stop there."

When they arrived, they all got out and ordered a coffee, which they brought to an outdoor table, and drank them in silence. Connie was thinking about their conversation with Tori and the email from

Cassie. Judging from her friends' thoughtful expressions, so were they.

"We'd better get going," Connie said. "Grace's shift ends in about an hour, and I don't want to keep her waiting."

As soon as they got back into Stephanie's car, her phone rang.

"It's Cassie," Stephanie said.

"I wonder why she's calling us," Elyse said. "We were just with her."

Stephanie started the engine so that the call would transmit over the car's bluetooth system.

"There's only one way to find out," Stephanie said as she accepted the call through a button on her steering wheel.

"Hi Cassie. I'm still with Elyse and Stephanie. We just stopped for coffee, and now we're on our way to Cathy's."

"I'm glad I caught the three of you together. I have some news. I just got off the phone with Andrea's father. He just spoke with the police, and they told him that the cause of Andrea's death was an overdose of Norpramin."

"Isn't that an antidepressant?" Stephanie asked.

"Yes," Cassie said. "Andrea's doctor had prescribed it to her. They ran a test on the coffee in Andrea's travel mug, and it was laced with a fatal dose. The medical examiner said that her symptoms were consistent with that finding. It looks like someone poisoned Andrea with her own prescription medication."

Chapter 12

CONNIE, ELYSE, AND STEPHANIE sat in silence after Cassie gave them the news.

"Are you still there?" Cassie asked.

"Sorry," Stephanie said. "We're here. I guess we're processing the news."

"It looks like our theory was correct," Connie said. "Between the time Andrea left her house at 8:00 on Monday morning until she met up with Jason for their kayaking date at 9:00, somebody gained access to her coffee and poisoned her."

"That explains why Jason didn't get sick," Stephanie said.

"But how would the killer have gained access to Cassie's Norpramin?" Elyse asked. "People usually keep their medications in their medicine cabinet or their nightstand."

"That makes Cathy look even more suspicious," Stephanie said. "She probably stole a bottle of pills while she was cleaning Andrea's bathroom."

"Not necessarily," Cassie said. "I happen to know that Andrea kept her prescription in her purse. She would sometimes forget to take it in the morning, so she got in the habit of carrying it with her. That way she could take it as soon as she remembered."

"Whoever killed her must have known that," Elyse said. "But that could be any one of our suspects – Calvin, Jeremy, Cathy. Anyone could have dumped the bottle of Norpramin, or a good portion of it, into her coffee."

"Don't forget Tori," Cassie said. "Her sweatshirt was in Andrea's office, so she was likely searching Andrea's emails the night of her death."

"And if Andrea went into Tori's house on Monday before she went kayaking, then Tori had access to Andrea's coffee and pills, as well," Connie said.

"This seems to vindicate Nate," Elyse said. "Since they only met once or twice, he likely wouldn't have known that she took Norpramin."

"That's true," Connie said. "But then again, the museum was broken into, and the letter was stolen containing his family's secret just after she was killed. I'm not sure how he could have done it, but he has the strongest motive. I say we keep him on the list."

"We should go and talk to Cathy so we can figure out what their 7:45 AM meeting was about. We should also talk to Shannon again sometime soon. Maybe she can shed some light on whether Andrea left her coffee and purse unattended at any time while Calvin and/or Jeremy were around."

"And don't forget, we need to talk to Nate," Cassie said.

Connie ran a hand through her hair. "Right. I don't know how we'll manage that."

"I'll see if I can think of something," Cassie said. "Let me know how it goes with Cathy."

"Will do," Stephanie said. Then she disconnected the call and drove the women to Cathy's house.

When they arrived at Cathy's, they knocked on her door. She answered right away, but disappointment spread across her face when she saw Connie, Stephanie, and Elyse.

"Hi," Stephanie said. "We're sorry to stop by unannounced, but something has come up in our investigation, and we needed to ask you a couple more questions."

"I already told you and the police everything I know. I don't have time right now. Please excuse me." Cathy started to close the door, but Connie stopped it with her hand.

"Why didn't you tell us about your meeting at 7:45 on Monday morning with Andrea?"

Cathy's jaw dropped. "How did you know about that? Did Andrea tell you what we talked about?"

Connie thought about how to best answer that question. The conversation could have been anything really, so she didn't want to guess at the topic. Instead, she tried to think of something general enough to encompass any problem. "She wasn't happy with you."

Cathy looked intently at Connie, then at the other two women. "You're right. The truth is, Andrea let me go on Monday morning, because she wasn't happy with my work. I told her that there were no hard feelings. She said we could make Monday my last day, since I was already there, so she paid me for the day then left to stop by the office. Everything else I told you was true. She came back after her errand to get her kayak, and I helped her load it onto the car. I wanted to show her that I wasn't angry about being fired. That was the last time I saw her. I didn't tell you before because I was embarrassed, and you had expressed interest in my cleaning your condo. But it doesn't matter now, because I've decided that I'm not taking on any new clients."

"I'm going to hold off on hiring a cleaning lady, anyway." Connie had almost forgotten she had said she was looking for a cleaning lady in order to get Cathy's contact information.

"Well, if that's all, I was in the middle of something."

There wasn't much left to say, so the women thanked her for her time and left.

"I don't buy her story," Connie said once they got back into Stephanie's car.

"Me, either," Elyse said. "We were just in Andrea's house, and it was sparkling clean. Cathy is obviously good at her job."

Connie nodded. "Cathy is hiding something for sure."

Stephanie called Cassie as they were driving home, and the women relayed their conversation with Cathy.

"Well," Cassie said, "Andrea *was* a bit of a perfectionist. But as far as cleaning ladies go, Cathy is pretty good. I don't think she would have fired her."

"And who knows if she fired her at all and what the real topic of their conversation was," Stephanie added. "She should definitely be at the top of our list of suspects."

A deep sigh came through Stephanie's phone.

"Hang in there, Cassie. We'll get to the bottom of this."

"I know. It's just that Andrea and I had made plans to get together on Wednesday. I had taken the day off from work, and we were planning to go kayaking, get a massage, and go out to lunch. We liked to spoil ourselves every so often. On those days, we would talk about everything that was going on in our lives. I only wish we had gotten together sooner. Then I might know the answers to some of these questions. I would know if she fired her cleaning lady, what was going on with the recliner, and we would have talked more about the letter and the desk. Not to mention that I might have some clue about why Tori's sweatshirt was in Andrea's office. Then maybe this mystery wouldn't be such a mystery."

"Try not to dwell on that," Stephanie said. "You couldn't have known."

The group agreed that their next task would be to talk to Shannon. Now that they knew that Andrea's cause of death was an overdose of Norpramin and that she kept it in her purse, they were hoping to get a better sense of who had access to it. So as not to be too conspicuous, they agreed that Connie and Stephanie should go to *Harold's Furniture* alone on Monday morning to find out what they could from Shannon.

They finished their conversation with Cassie just as they were approaching the downtown area.

"Let's all meet up at *Surfside Restaurant* on Monday night so you can fill me in on what happens when you talk with Shannon," Elyse suggested.

"Let's put that off until after Connie's banana boat outing with Zach and his parents," Stephanie said, laughing. "I want to hear all about that day, as well."

"How about drinks and appetizers after I close the store on Wednesday?"

Elyse tapped on her phone. "It's on my calendar."

Stephanie parked her car in the lot at the end of Connie's street, where Elyse had left her car. Elyse drove off, but Stephanie had decided to pop in and say hello to Gallagher, so she and Connie walked down the street together.

"See you on Wednesday night," Connie said as Stephanie headed into *Gallagher's Tropical Shack* with a smile as big as the Gulf of Mexico.

Chapter 13

ON SUNDAY MORNING at the 7:00 Mass, Connie scanned Our Lady, Star of the Sea Church to see if Zach and his parents were there, but they must have been going to a later Mass. She didn't blame them for wanting to sleep in.

The morning passed slowly. Grace arrived at *Just Jewelry* at 10:30 with two coffees in hand, a habit that Connie immensely appreciated, and at 12:45, Zach strolled in with his parents.

Pauline embraced Connie, and Zach introduced his parents to Grace.

"Come on," Connie said to Ben and Pauline. "I'll give you a tour of the store." She began with the Fair Trade section, where Connie described her previous work with a non-profit called *Feeding the Hungry*. It took her a while to figure out a way to combine her passion for jewelry making, which she learned while volunteering in Africa after college, with her passion for humanitarian work. "This store just seemed like the perfect fit."

Zach put his arm around Connie's shoulders. "I'm grateful that she figured out a way. Otherwise, we wouldn't be together."

"It's a lovely shop," Pauline said. "Your family must be as proud of you as we are of Zach. He works hard, but he loves his job."

Grace smiled warmly at Pauline and Ben. "I've been a friend of the Petretta family for more than ten years, and I can already tell that the two of you would enjoy meeting Connie's parents."

Ben returned her smile. "I'm sure we would. Hopefully, we'll have the opportunity in the near future."

"We don't want to take up too much of your time," Pauline said. "We just wanted to stop in to say hello and tell you that we are looking forward to our banana boat ride on Wednesday morning. You are a doll for setting that up, Connie."

"What are your plans for today?" Grace asked.

"We're going shopping this morning." Pauline chuckled. "Well, I am. The boys are coming along to humor me."

"Have a great time," Connie said.

Zach turned toward Connie as they were heading out the door. "We'll pick you up at Palm Paradise at 9:45 on Wednesday morning."

"Sounds good. I'll be downstairs and ready to go."

"And be careful today when you meet with Francis," Zach said. "Make sure you stay in a public place."

Connie mock-saluted him. "Will do."

After they left, Connie glanced at the time on her cell phone.

"It must be nearly time to leave for your meeting with Francis," Grace said.

"Yes, we're meeting at 1:30. I should head over now."

"Be careful," Grace said. "I'll look forward to hearing how it goes. And don't rush to get back. I don't have any plans this afternoon, so I can stay here as long as you need me."

"You're the best, Grace."

Connie arrived at *Callaway's Restaurant* just before 1:30. The outdoor patio was crowded, but the bar was virtually empty. A distinguished-looking man with grey hair and dark eyes looked up when Connie entered the bar. His expectant expression vanished when he saw that it was Connie. He sighed and looked at his gold wristwatch.

The few other patrons in the bar area were either part of a couple or a group, so Connie guessed that the gentleman was Francis. She smiled and slowly walked to the table where he was sitting. She dreaded having to tell him that Concetta had passed away.

The man looked up and smiled politely.

"Are you Francis?"

He stood and gave Connie a confused look. "Yes, I am."

"My name is Connie Petretta. Concetta Belmonte was my aunt."

His kind eyes filled with sadness. "*Was* your aunt?"

A lump formed in Connie's throat "Yes. Unfortunately, Aunt Concetta passed away a little over two years ago."

Tears moistened Francis' eyes.

"I'm sorry to be the one to give you the news. I live in Aunt Concetta's condo now, so your letter came to my home. Since there wasn't a return address on the envelope, I opened it."

"I'm glad you did," Francis said. He studied her for a moment. "I should have guessed you were related. I can see the resemblance."

Connie smiled. She and her aunt had shared the same olive skin and dark eyes. Even though Concetta's style was more glamorous than Connie's, she always loved it when people noticed their resemblance.

Francis gestured for Connie to sit in the navy blue booth, on the other side of the small, circular marble table.

As soon as Connie sat down, the waiter came over.

"Just an iced tea for me, please. I have to go back to work later."

Francis tapped his crystal glass. "Another bourbon for me." He gazed past Connie, as if he were recovering his emotions, then returned his attention to her. "It's been more than forty years since I've seen Concetta."

Connie told Francis about Concetta's final illness and highlighted some of the major events in her life and career. Francis said he had followed Concetta's Hollywood acting career, so he was aware of the details of her life that had been public information. But he was interested to hear about it from Connie's perspective.

After Connie filled Francis in on all of the details of her aunt's life that seemed appropriate to share, he leaned back in his chair and studied Connie. "You're probably wondering how I knew your aunt."

Connie smiled. "Yes, I am."

"Concetta and I dated in high school. We loved each other, but my mother put a lot of pressure on me to marry someone from, let's just say a more economically prosperous family. In fact, she had a very specific young woman in mind. Concetta and I talked about running away together to Hollywood and getting married. As our high school graduation approached, my mother made it increasingly difficult for me to see Concetta. The day of our graduation, Concetta wrote me a note saying she was leaving for Hollywood the following week. She included an airline ticket and asked me to meet her at the airport. My mother found the note and ticket before I did and tore them both up." He smiled. "Those were the days when airline tickets were made of paper."

Francis swallowed hard and looked down to compose himself. "I can't imagine how Concetta must have felt when I didn't show up at Logan Airport. Since I thought she left without saying a word to me, I believed that she didn't love me anymore. I was heartbroken, but I eventually married Samantha, the woman my mother wanted me to marry all along. Don't get me wrong, we had a good life. But I'm not sure I ever forgave my mother for taking that choice away. By the time I learned what happened, Samantha and I had built a life together, and I knew that Concetta had married, as well, so I thought it was best to leave it alone. When Samantha passed away last year, I thought I'd make my peace with Concetta. But it looks like I was too late."

It was strange to hear about a part of Concetta's life that Connie knew nothing about. In a way, it made her feel closer to her aunt. She felt badly that her aunt had to endure that heartache. Concetta's marriage didn't end well, so maybe her life would have been different if Concetta had married Francis. "I'm so sorry that you lost each other over a misunderstanding, Francis," Connie said.

Francis was eager to learn more about Concetta's life, so they ordered appetizers and talked for more than an hour. Connie filled Francis in on the things he couldn't have known from the headlines. He turned out to be a charming man. The more she learned about him, the easier it was to imagine Francis and Concetta together. And it seemed like he would have made a good uncle.

Francis remembered Josephine, Connie's mother, and was happy to hear about what became of her, as well. Connie even had a bunch of family photos on her phone, including many with Concetta, so she forwarded a few to Francis.

"My aunt had a very forgiving heart," Connie said. "She didn't have a bitter bone in her body. I'm sure she didn't hold what happened against you."

Francis smiled and nodded. "I'm sure you're right. I would have liked to have explained it to her myself, but I feel like this was the next best thing."

"I think about her every day," Connie said. "Thank you for sharing your story with me. It makes me feel closer to her."

"I'm glad Concetta had so many people in her life who loved her."

He glanced at his wristwatch and his eyes flew wide open. "I didn't mean to keep you so long. I should let you get back to work."

"You're probably right. It's been a wonderful afternoon. I almost feel as though Concetta is sitting with us." Connie stood up, handed Francis a business card, and gave him a hug. "My cell phone number and email address are on here. If you're ever back in town, please reach out."

He smiled. "I certainly will."

Before leaving the restaurant, Connie decided to go to the ladies' room. When she turned around, she saw a flurrying motion out of the corner of her eye. Two familiar-looking men slumped down in their chairs and whipped their menus in front of their faces. But Connie would recognize that blond hair anywhere.

"Zach?" Connie asked, walking toward them. They slowly lowered their menus, and Zach and his father stood to greet Connie. They were sitting on the same side of the table, both facing the direction of the bar.

Connie walked over to where the Hughes men were sitting, still slightly confused. "Did you know I was over there?"

Zach and Ben looked at one another uncomfortably.

Then it dawned on Connie. "You came to watch me, didn't you?"

"Don't be mad at Zach," Ben said. "We were just concerned for your safety. Not that you can't take care of yourself, but we just thought 'better safe than sorry.'"

Connie hugged them both. "I appreciate the concern. It was very sweet of you."

Both men breathed a sigh of relief.

"It looked like you were having a good meeting," Zach said. "We almost left halfway through, once we realized you were okay."

"But by then, we had already seen the menu and wanted to order lunch."

"It was a wonderful meeting. It almost felt like Aunt Concetta was alive again."

"I'm so happy for you, Connie," Ben said. "I'm glad it worked out."

"Can you join us for dessert?" Zach asked.

"I'd love to, but I'd better get back to the shop so Grace can leave. Her shift ended more than an hour ago."

On her way back to *Just Jewelry*, Connie called her mother and recounted her conversation with Francis.

"I can't believe something this huge happened to my sister and I never knew about it."

"I know. I felt the same way at first. But I enjoyed talking about Auntie Concetta, and Francis clearly loved hearing about her life."

"And that was so sweet of Zach and his father to have your back like that."

Connie felt a smile spread across her face. "I know. It really was. I think you and Dad are going to like the Hughes."

"I'm sure we will, honey. Are there any major life events that might be coming up soon where we might have the chance to meet them?"

"Mom!"

Connie could feel her mother's smile across the fifteen-hundred miles that separated them.

"Okay, I'll stop. But at least text me Ben's phone number. I'd like to thank him personally for watching out for my little girl. If the two of you aren't going to bring us together for any celebrations soon, I might as well call and thank him."

"All right," Connie said. "I'll get it from Zach and text you. I've gotta run. I just parked my car, and I have to get back to work."

Chapter 14

THE FOLLOWING DAY the store received little foot traffic, which was typical for Mondays. So, since Grace worked on Monday mornings, it was easy for Connie to break away with Stephanie, as planned.

Connie picked up Stephanie at her home at 10:00, and they drove to *Harold's Furniture* to talk with Shannon. Fortunately, Stephanie was able to arrange her work schedule so that she would be in between clients at that time.

Stephanie was just pulling into her driveway when Connie arrived. "I was afraid I'd be late. My previous appointment was clear across town," she said after slipping into Connie's car.

It was a little before 10:30 when the two women arrived at *Harold's Furniture*. Shannon was finishing with a customer, so Connie and Stephanie pretended to browse the merchandise while they waited.

Jonathan, the sales associate they had met last Monday, tried to assist Connie and Stephanie, making the logical assumption that they were there to buy furniture, but Stephanie told him that Shannon had been helping them and they preferred to wait for her.

He tried to hide his disappointment with a friendly smile.

While they were talking to Jonathan, Connie noticed that the defective recliners were still on the floor.

When Shannon finished with her customer, Jonathan whispered something in her ear, and she walked over to where Connie and Stephanie were standing. Shannon glanced around to be sure nobody was within earshot. "I'm happy to see you two. The police told us that Andrea's death is now officially a murder investigation. I just can't believe it."

"That's why we're here," Connie said. "We heard the same thing and were hoping you might be able to answer a few more questions."

"I don't know what information I could possibly give you," Shannon said. "I have no idea who did this."

Stephanie pretended to be admiring a coffee table while Connie asked the questions, but they didn't need to pretend to be shopping. Nobody was paying much attention to them, anyway.

"We know that Andrea was killed by an overdose of Norpramin and that the lethal dose was in her coffee," Connie said. "We also know that she stopped here the morning she died."

"That's right," Shannon said. "Wait, does that mean that someone *here* poisoned her coffee?" She glanced nervously at her colleagues. "Please tell me that's not what happened."

"That's what we're trying to figure out," Connie said. "Andrea was also in contact with other people the morning of her death."

Shannon breathed a sigh of relief, but concern remained on her face.

"Andrea used to keep her Norpramin prescription in her purse," Connie continued, "so the killer likely used her own medication to kill her. Think back to Monday morning. Do you remember if Andrea left her purse and coffee mug unattended at any time, and if so, who would have had access?"

Stephanie looked up from the coffee table she had been fake-admiring and focused her attention on Shannon.

"Let me think," Shannon said. "Andrea arrived about 8:30 that morning. She was carrying that stainless steel travel mug that she brought every day. I didn't think much of it at the time until the police asked about it. I wish I knew what had been in it. I would have smashed it on the ground."

"What did she do after she came in?"

"I teased her about coming into the store on her first day of vacation, jokingly telling her she should get a life. She laughed and said she was only here for a quick meeting with Calvin and Jeremy. Then she walked down the hall and into Calvin's office."

"How long was she in there?" Stephanie asked.

"About ten minutes. Then Jeremy left. He said he had an appointment to meet with a supplier across town and he was already late."

"So, at this point, Calvin and Andrea were alone in Calvin's office?" Connie asked.

"Yes, they must have been. Wait a minute! After Jeremy left, Andrea went into the ladies' room. I remember, because we went in at the same time. She seemed upset, so I asked if she was okay. She splashed some water on her face and said that she was fine."

"Did she have her coffee at that point?" Connie asked.

"No, she didn't have anything with her – not her purse *or* her coffee mug."

"Are you *sure*?" Stephanie asked.

"Yes, I'm positive. We walked out together, but she went back to Calvin's office while I came back to the showroom. A few minutes later, she left the store with her coffee mug and purse in hand."

"That means Calvin was alone with both Andrea's purse, which likely contained her bottle of Norpramin, and her coffee," Connie said.

"Do you think he would have had enough time to crush the pills and put them in her coffee?" Stephanie asked.

"It would be cutting it close, but I suppose he could have if he had it planned out," Shannon said, with fresh fear in her eyes. "Oh no! I might work for a killer. I need to find another job."

Connie place her hand on Shannon's forearm. "Don't do anything rash. Just because he had a motive and a possible opportunity doesn't mean he killed Andrea."

Jonathan looked over at the three women.

Stephanie noticed his glance at the same time Connie did, so she went back to fawning over the coffee table. After pretending to ask Shannon a few more questions about coffee tables and end tables and snapping a few pictures for good measure, Connie and Stephanie thanked Shannon for her time and left.

"You know, it wasn't a *total* act," Stephanie said as they walked toward Connie's Jetta. "I really did like that coffee table."

"But you already have such beautiful furniture in your bungalow."

Stephanie looped her arm through Connie's. "I know. Get me out of here before I spend money on things I don't need."

When they got back to Stephanie's house, she invited Connie inside for a glass of iced tea.

Connie glanced at the time on her phone. "Maybe just a quick glass. Then I have to get back to *Just Jewelry*."

Stephanie disappeared into the kitchen and returned a couple of minutes later with two tall glasses. She handed one to Connie, and they headed out to the lanai.

"I like yours better than the one you were admiring at *Harold's*," Connie said, stopping in front of Stephanie's coffee table on the way out.

Stephanie tilted her head and studied her marble coffee table. "So do I."

Connie settled into the outdoor sofa, and Stephanie took the seat facing her. She looked around at the potted palms and brightly colored flowers scattered throughout the lanai. "It gets more beautiful every time I come out here." Connie thought of her balcony, which contained only one plant stand with only a few herbs and potted flowers. "Your lanai puts my balcony to shame. It looks like a lush tropical rain forest out here."

They quietly sipped their tea for a few minutes, each lost in her own thoughts. Then Stephanie broke the silence. "I guess we should move Calvin to the top of our suspect list."

"It looks that way. He wasn't alone for that long with her purse and mug, but he could have acted quickly. And we can cross off Jeremy. He never had access to Andrea's coffee and purse on Monday morning, so he couldn't have done it."

"At least we made some progress today. I'll call Elyse and Cassie and fill them in on our conversation with Shannon. I have a twenty minute drive to my next client, so it will give me something to do," Stephanie said.

"That sounds like a plan." Connie placed her empty glass on the end table. "I'd better get back to work. I hate to leave Grace alone in the store when I don't need to."

"I'll see you Wednesday night at *Surfside*. Have fun banana boating with Zach and his parents."

Chapter 15

SINCE CONNIE WAS ALONE in the store on Tuesdays, she stayed busy serving customers and making jewelry in preparation for the upcoming busy season.

On Wednesday morning, Connie woke up early so she could take Ginger for a long walk and have a leisurely mug of tea before Zach and his parents picked her up at 9:45 for their banana boat excursion. Then she changed into a bathing suit, threw on her beach cover up, and waited for them downstairs.

Connie had observed banana boats full of squealing passengers speeding along the coastline many times while walking the beach. She had it in the back of her mind that she would like to try it someday, but she never quite got around to it. Even though Zach ribbed his mother about her new adventurous streak, Connie was glad that Pauline had suggested it.

Zach arrived with his parents right on time. Pauline wore a broad smile that reminded Connie of a child who was about to be set free in a candy store. Zach and his father seemed amused as they listened to Pauline chatter away about their upcoming adventure. Even though Connie had only met Zach's parents a couple of times, she already felt comfortable in their presence.

"We were hoping you would let us buy you an early lunch after banana boating," Ben said.

"Connie might have to get back to work," Zach said.

"It's okay. I got coverage until the early afternoon. I'd love to join you for lunch."

"Wonderful," Pauline said.

Zach smiled gratefully at Connie through the rearview mirror.

They parked in a lot downtown, since *Sapphire Beach Boat Rentals* was close to that area and the weather-beaten pier that stretched toward the horizon.

When they arrived, Travis and Ashley were ready for them. They had brought the twin banana boat down to the water, where it sat attached to a jet ski.

Connie introduced Travis and Ashley to Zach's parents.

After the introductions, Travis handed everyone a life vest. "Required wearing."

"Solid idea," Zach said.

"Now don't you worry," Travis said to Ben and Pauline. "It's only the four of you on this excursion, and I won't go any faster than you are comfortable going. We'll be out there for about twenty-five minutes, and I will keep checking with you to see how fast you want to go."

"Oh, you can go *really* fast," Pauline said. "We're here for a thrill ride."

Zach and his father looked at one another again and chuckled.

"I'm beginning to like this new daring side of you, Mom."

"Twenty-five minutes might not seem long," Travis continued, "but you'll be surprised how tired you will be, even though the jet ski is doing all the hard work. It will give your core quite the workout."

Starting with Pauline, Travis got them each situated on the banana boat. "Rest your feet here," he said, pointing to the laterally flanking tubes. "In addition to stabilizing the boat, these will also help you stay balanced."

Since it was a double banana boat, Zach's parents sat next to one another in the front while Connie and Zach sat side by side behind them. Once everyone was in place, Travis took his seat on the jet ski, turned on the engine, and slowly drove away from the shore.

The wind pushed back Connie's dark hair, and the refreshing gulf water gently splashed on everyone.

As they picked up speed, Travis glanced back to check on them.

Pauline gave him a thumbs up. "You can go faster."

Encouraged by the laughter of his four passengers, Travis gradually accelerated the boat.

After about ten minutes of cruising down the coastline, Travis slowed down.

"Is everything okay?" Zach asked.

"Absolutely." Travis pointed to two dolphins playing off to the side, with the sapphire waters dancing behind them. "I didn't want you to miss those fellows."

Pauline squealed with delight at the playful creatures, who seemed to be taking pleasure in entertaining them.

Connie glanced over at Zach, who was wearing a wide smile as he watched his parents enjoying themselves. His joy was contagious, and she was happy to be sharing this moment with him.

When they started moving again, Connie scanned the shoreline and realized that they were approaching the area where it was likely that Andrea had died and Jason had experienced what had to be one of the most traumatizing events of his life. The memory of finding Andrea's body floating in on a kayak dimmed her spirits.

Zach must have noticed Connie's expression. He reached over and gave her hand a squeeze. Before she had too much time to dwell on it, Travis turned the boat around and headed back towards the pier.

By the time Travis slowed down his jet ski and brought them back to shore, Connie was smiling again.

Travis helped Pauline and Ben off the boat.

"I'm so glad you suggested this, Mom," Zach said. "That was a lot of fun."

"I am, too," Pauline said. "But Travis was right. I'll be sore tomorrow."

Ben patted his stomach. "Lunch is going to taste all the better, too."

Before they left, Pauline handed Travis her phone and requested that he take a picture of the four of them in front of the banana boat. After taking Connie's number, she promised to send Connie the photo.

After Zach paid for the excursion, they decided to go to *Gallagher's.* Zach thought his parents would enjoy the thatched roof and tropical atmosphere.

When Gallagher spotted Connie and Zach, he came over to say hello. Since he had been dating Stephanie, Gallagher became fast friends with Zach and Josh.

Gallagher excused himself after hearing from Pauline all about their adventure. "I'd better get back to work. I'm buried in paperwork back there. But I'm so glad I got to meet you."

He smiled and left just as their server came to take their drink order. But first, Gallagher whispered something in her ear. A couple of minutes later, their server brought over a big plate of nachos. "It's on the house," she said. "It's a welcome gift from Gallagher."

"What a sweetie," Pauline said. "Everyone has been treating us like family all week."

"These look delicious," Zach said, filling his plate.

"Zach tells us that you and Elyse were there when the victim's body in his current investigation was discovered," Ben said.

Connie filled her own plate, as well. "Yes. We were with another friend on the beach when a kayak drifted ashore. At first, we thought the rider was just sunbathing, but eventually, we realized that something was wrong. The victim's name was Andrea."

"How awful for all of you," Pauline said.

Ben let out a chuckle. "We also hear that you often find yourself intertwined in our son's investigations."

Connie glanced at Zach, who was trying to suppress a smirk. Unsuccessfully.

"I guess you could say that. Murder investigations seem to follow me ever since I moved to Sapphire Beach. I try to stay out of them, but I somehow always end up right in the middle."

Zach's smirk turned into a chuckle.

Even Connie couldn't look Zach straight in the eyes when she said that. It was a gigantic stretch of the truth to imply that she did her best to stay out of Zach's investigations. The truth was, she couldn't seem to stay away. Whenever she had even the slightest connection to a case, she felt compelled to dig deeper. And digging deeper usually led to an all-out investigation.

"My heart goes out to poor Stephanie," Connie said. "She was friends with the victim. I can't imagine seeing someone I know in that state."

"That must have been terrible." Then Pauline looked thoughtfully at Connie. "But I can see why you would be pulled into these cases. A murder investigation *does* sound like quite the adventure."

"Don't even *think* of it, Mom," Zach said.

Pauline waved away her son's comment. "Banana boating is enough excitement for this week. Don't worry, I have no intention of causing trouble."

"Zach and Josh will find the killer," Connie said. "They always do."

"Don't let Connie fool you. I'm sure she's knee-deep in her own investigation at this point," Zach said. "Since she won't listen to me and stay out of things, we have an arrangement. She promises to tell me if she's ever in any danger, and I don't give her too hard a time about her sleuthing."

"So, who's your favorite suspect in this case?" Ben asked Connie.

"It's hard to say." Connie tried to downplay the extent of her involvement. She especially didn't want to mention that Cassie let her into Andrea's condo, where they found Tori's sweatshirt and an incriminating email to Cathy. Or that they had been to *Harold's Furniture* twice, and Calvin was her prime suspect. Zach might see these as crossing a line.

"It could be connected to a museum where the victim volunteered. There was a letter…"

Zach interrupted her. "Whoa, that's not public information. I don't know how you find these things out, Connie, but you never know who could be listening."

Connie pretended to zip her lips and throw away the key. She decided the best course of action was to change the subject. "How much longer will the two of you be in town?"

"Unfortunately, we are leaving tomorrow morning. We want to get back for our grandson's soccer tournament, so it's a quick visit this time."

"Hopefully, you can stay longer the next time," Connie said.

"We hope so, too," Pauline said.

After a leisurely lunch, they drove Connie home.

Zach's parents got out of the car to say goodbye to Connie.

"I had a great time," Connie said, giving them each a hug.

As Zach's father hugged Connie back, he said to Zach, "Don't let her get away."

"Not a chance," Zach said, putting his arm around Connie's shoulders and walking her to the lobby.

Chapter 16

AFTER CHANGING into her favorite black and white sundress, Connie fastened Ginger's leash and headed into work. Since there was an available spot at a meter right in front of *Just Jewelry*, she parked there for the time being.

Grace was having lunch at the oak table, so Connie grabbed a water from the fridge out back and filled Grace in on her banana boat excursion with the Hughes. "They are so nice. I don't know why I was so stressed about meeting them."

Grace winked. "It's because you care so much about their son."

Connie's cheeks grew warm. "I guess that's why."

Within no time, it was 2:00, which was Grace's usual quitting time. Connie spent the rest of the afternoon and evening creating jewelry and tending to customers. She hadn't brought dinner, since she had gone out to lunch and was meeting Stephanie and Elyse for drinks and appetizers after work. By the time the evening rolled round, she was getting hungry.

About 8:00, she received a text from Stephanie. *I have some news on the case. I'll tell you when I see you tonight.*

When it was time to close up shop, Connie took Ginger for a quick walk, then dropped her off at Palm Paradise and headed to one of her favorite restaurants, *Surfside*. On some evenings, they had live music, which usually included a man with a guitar covering hits from the sixties and seventies. But it was probably better that there was no entertainment tonight, since the women wanted to talk.

By the time Connie arrived, Elyse and Stephanie were already seated at a table near the edge of the deck overlooking the water. Perfect. She could already feel the stress leaving her body.

When their server came, Connie ordered her usual - a frozen pina colada. Since she was hungry for more than appetizers, she also decided to order a grouper sandwich and sweet potato fries.

"So," Connie said to Stephanie, "I've been dying to know what you've found out about the case."

"I was hoping we could talk about your day with Zach and his parents first. The suspense is killing me."

"We went banana boating. We had a blast. His parents are great. Now tell us about your news!"

Stephanie laughed. "I guess that sums it up. Okay, well remember how Tori, Andrea's neighbor, had a sore shoulder when we talked with her outside Andrea's house?"

Connie and Elyse nodded.

"Well, I heard from a coworker that Tori had to have physical therapy, because she was in a car accident."

"What does that have to do with Andrea?" Elyse asked.

"I'm getting to that. Apparently, she hit a neighbor's car and didn't report it."

"I'm still not making the connection with Andrea," Elyse said.

"It involves Andrea, because she saw the whole thing. Tori had had a couple of drinks and got behind the wheel. Andrea saw her crash into the neighbor's parked car and Tori begged Andrea not to report her to the neighbor. But you can't tell anyone about that. My colleague only told me, because she knew I was friends with Andrea and that we are investigating her death."

"Did Andrea ever tell the neighbor what she saw?" Elyse asked.

"Tori doesn't know if Andrea reported the incident before her death. Tori was trying to plead her case with Andrea, saying how humiliating it would be if her drinking problem became public, especially as a high school principal. It could even mean losing her job. She said the neighbor is wealthy, so the car repairs wouldn't be a hardship. But Tori didn't actually *know* if Andrea reported her to the neighbor."

"That's probably why Tori was in Andrea's office on Monday night," Connie said. "She must have hacked into Andrea's email account to see if she could find any clues about whether Andrea told the neighbor."

"Well, that certainly provides her with a motive," Elyse said.

"We need to talk to Tori again," Connie said.

"I agree. We know where she lives. Let's pick an evening and stop by," Stephanie said.

"How about tomorrow at 6:00?" Connie suggested. "Abby will be working, and she can cover my 7:00 jewelry-making class if I run late."

Stephanie and Elyse agreed.

All three women quickly forgot about the case when their food arrived.

"We need to set another day to hang out, since our day at the beach was a bust," Elyse said.

Stephanie took one of Connie's sweet potato fries. "You're right. But I don't know if I can get another day off so soon. Some of my colleagues are on vacation."

"How about Sunday?" Elyse suggested. "I'll probably have an open house in the morning, but I should be able to join you in the afternoon. That way Stephanie doesn't have to take a day off."

"I can do that," Connie said. "I'm sure Abby can come in early, or maybe Grace will stay. I'll double check, but count me in."

"It's a plan, then," Elyse said.

Connie pushed away her empty plate. "Let's take a walk on the beach so I can work off some of these French fries."

The women paid their bill and walked down the wooden stairs leading to the soft white sand.

After a few minutes of silence, Elyse looked at Connie and smirked. "Spill it, Connie. I know that look. What are you thinking about?"

"I was thinking about Nate. He *had* to be the one who stole the letter from the museum. He was at least behind it. So, we know he will go to extremes in order to protect his family's secret. I don't think it's a huge leap to think he might commit murder."

"But, as far as we know, Andrea didn't meet with him last Monday morning. He wouldn't have had access to Andrea's pills or coffee," Elyse said.

"True," Connie said. "But you never know. He could have followed Andrea to the parking lot, and while Jason and Andrea were transporting their kayaks to the water, he could have slipped some poison into her coffee."

"I don't know," Stephanie said. "How would he know that she had the Norpramin in her purse? And it would have taken longer than that for the drug to kick in. It seems like a stretch."

"I didn't say I had it all figured out. But Jason *did* say that a boat pulled up to their kayaks, and its driver knocked him out so he couldn't get help for Andrea. So, whoever killed Andrea was obviously in the area, watching and making sure that their plan was successful. Maybe the killer wasn't one of the people who Andrea met with that morning. Maybe the killer was following her and waiting for his or her opportunity. Nate would fit that bill. I don't know exactly how or when he would have accessed her coffee mug and pills, but it's not out of the realm of possibility."

"I suppose it's not impossible," Elyse said. "Although it seems more likely that one of the people that Andrea met with that morning - Calvin, Cathy, or Tori - would have done it."

"I agree, but I'm still not ready to take Nate off the list, especially since he probably broke into the museum," Connie said. "He committed one crime over this letter. I'm not convinced he didn't commit a second, even worse, one. I want to talk to him."

"Why don't we think about a possible plan and regroup in the next day or two," Stephanie suggested.

The others agreed.

After a few more minutes, the women decided to call it a night.

On Thursday morning, Connie woke up early to go for a swim in the gulf before work. She was hoping to clear her head, since she had tossed and turned all night, thinking about the case. Then she walked Ginger and headed downtown to open the store.

Grace was already there when Connie arrived. They sat in the store's seating area, and Connie filled her in on what they had learned so far, assuring Grace that she was keeping her promise and not letting Stephanie put herself in any dangerous situations.

"It sounds like you need to learn more about Nate," Grace said. "He's the only one of your suspects you haven't talked to yet."

"He is. But I don't even know his last name or where to find him."

"Maybe Cassie would know," Grace said.

"I don't know why I didn't think of that. I'll give her a call. In the meantime, hopefully we will learn something when we talk to Tori tonight."

Since there weren't any customers in the store yet, Connie called Cassie.

"Hi Cassie, would you be able to get me Nate's full name? I know his mother is a Cartwright, but I don't know Nate's last name."

"Sure, that's easy. I don't even have to look it up. It's Thompson."

"Do you know anything else about him?"

"Only that he has a boat over at the marina where he spends all of his free time. Other than that, I don't know a whole lot about him. I figured you ruled him out since he didn't have access to Andrea's coffee or pills."

"I haven't ruled him out completely, even though I don't know how he could have done it. I'd love to talk to him. Do you know how I could 'accidentally run into him?'"

"He spends a lot of his time at the yacht club, but you won't be able to get in without a membership. My father stores his boat there, so we are all members. I could come with you."

169

"Won't Nate recognize you from the museum if you're with me?"

"I doubt Nate is even aware that I volunteer at the museum. He'll never make the connection. I'll ask my father about his routine so we can maximize our chances of seeing him, and I'll let you know what I learn."

"Sounds like a plan," Connie said.

Chapter 17

AFTER LUNCH, Connie decided to take Ginger for a walk before Grace left for the day. When Connie grabbed the leash from its hook in the storage room, the dog perked up in her doggie bed, which was tucked away in the back of the store.

"We'll be right back," Connie said, as she and Ginger headed out the door and toward the beach.

Connie and Ginger stopped at *Friendly Scoops* to say hi to Emily, the owner of the best ice cream shop in town. Emily always kept a doggie bowl filled with water outside her shop for the four-legged residents of Sapphire Beach.

Emily was sitting at one of the round, cafe-style, wrought iron tables taking a break when Connie and Ginger arrived.

"Can I join you?" Connie asked.

"Of course. I was just resting up for the mid-afternoon rush."

Suddenly, an ominous feeling washed over Connie. She glanced over her shoulder, then at the people strolling down the street.

"What is it?" Emily asked.

"Probably nothing. I just got an eerie feeling that someone is watching me."

"That's creepy," Emily said.

"It just came over me like a wave." Connie shrugged her shoulders. "I'm sure it's nothing."

Emily looked around. "I don't see anyone, but you have good instincts. I wouldn't go anywhere alone until the feeling passes."

"That's probably a good idea," Connie said. "How is business?"

"It's picking up a little, now that the snowbirds are returning."

"Same with my shop."

There was a brief lull in the conversation while Emily studied Connie's expression.

"Now *you're* creeping me out," Connie said.

"I'm just wondering why someone would be following you. Wait a minute. You're involved in another investigation, aren't you?"

Connie leaned back in the wrought iron chair. "Well, sort of."

Emily chuckled. "I should have guessed it when I saw on the news that a local woman was found murdered in her kayak."

"That's the one. Her name was Andrea Fontaine. I was with my friends, Stephanie and Elyse, at the beach when the kayak containing her body drifted ashore. We were the ones who found it. The victim was a friend of Stephanie's."

"In that case, you really do need to be vigilant. A killer could be following you."

Ginger hopped onto Connie's lap, and Emily scratched the top of the dog's head. "She's a sweet dog, but I wouldn't exactly call her a ferocious protector."

Connie smiled at Ginger, who raised her floppy ears and looked up at her with big brown eyes. "You'd be surprised. She's inadvertently assisted me in a few jams."

"It's such a beautiful day. I'd love to sit here talking all afternoon, but I'd better get back to work. I have to cover for my employee so she can take a break before it gets busy."

"Same here," Connie said. "I just wanted to stop by and say hello."

After leaving *Friendly Scoops*, Connie weaved in and out of the streets that ran perpendicular to the beach, so she could give Ginger some exercise while avoiding the sand. She had just given her a bath and didn't feel like doing it again so soon.

As Connie turned the corner and headed down the street, the feeling of being followed returned. Connie turned her head sharply. There was a couple who appeared to be in their seventies holding hands and passersby window shopping, but nobody looked out of place.

Maybe it's my imagination. Or maybe the person ducked into a store.

Connie briefly observed Ginger. The dog seemed oblivious to any possible danger, which was a good sign. She back-tracked and glanced through the windows as she passed the various shops, but she didn't see anyone she recognized, and nobody appeared to be trying to hide from her view.

As Connie and Ginger continued their walk, the uneasy feeling disappeared.

"I guess it really was my imagination," she said to Ginger. "I must be paranoid."

After making a quick detour to buy two coffees, she checked the meter in her car, which was parked on the street in front of *Just Jewelry*. Forty minutes still remained, so Connie decided to enjoy her coffee before moving her car to the parking lot so she wouldn't be running out all day to feed the meter.

Connie handed Grace one of the coffees, and the ladies brought them into the store's seating area. Connie sat on the red sofa, where she had a clear view of the door, and Grace sat on an armchair facing her.

Connie was just about to ask Grace about her afternoon plans, since her shift was nearly over, when Grace stood abruptly and marched over to the front window.

"What's wrong?" Connie asked, following behind her.

"I think you just got a parking ticket. Look, there's an envelope on your windshield."

"That's impossible," Connie said. "I still have plenty of time left on my meter. I just checked it."

They stepped outside, and Connie looked up and down the street, but there was no sign of a meter maid.

"Look," Grace said, nodding toward a white envelope tucked beneath one of Connie's windshield wipers.

Connie lifted the wiper and opened the envelope.

There was a piece of paper inside that read: *I'm watching you. Watch your step.*

Connie's heart sank - not so much because she was afraid of the note's author, but because it meant she had to tell Zach she had been threatened. There was no way around it, especially since Grace also saw the note.

Within fifteen minutes, Zach was in her shop, sitting at the table across from Connie and Grace.

Connie handed him the note and told him about the uneasy feeling she had while walking Ginger.

Grace abruptly turned her chair toward Connie. "You didn't tell me about that."

"To be honest, I forgot all about it by the time I got our coffees and returned to the store."

Grace's eyes suddenly flew wide open, and a worried expression spread across her face. She excused herself, pulled out her cell phone, and marched out back. Connie presumed she was calling Stephanie to make sure she was okay.

"Who have you talked to that might feel threatened by your questions?" Zach asked.

"We spoke with Cathy, Calvin, and Tori, Andrea's neighbor." She decided not to mention their plans to talk with Nate or their planned second conversation with Tori. After all, Zach only asked who they had *already* talked to.

Zach did his best not to react, but she could see the frustration in his eyes. He swallowed hard. "Okay, I'll look into it. But in the meantime, stay alert. And tell your partners in crime the same thing."

Then he kissed her on the top of the head and left.

She hated to cause more work for Zach, but she knew he couldn't get too angry, since he didn't want her to hesitate to contact him when she had information or was potentially in danger.

By the time Zach left, Connie's phone had already blown up with messages from Stephanie and Elyse. Connie had to laugh. Grace probably called Stephanie, who in turn likely filled in Elyse.

Connie assured them that all was well but told them about Zach's warning.

While she was texting with Elyse and Stephanie, she also received a text from Cassie.

My father said that Nate usually takes his boat out in the afternoon, then goes to the bar at the yacht club for drinks. He said he's usually there by 5:00. Are you free tomorrow night?

Since she wanted to tell Cassie about the threatening note she received, Connie called her back rather than reply with a text.

"Hi, Cassie. I could come tomorrow night. Abby will be coming in for her shift about 4:00, so any time after that."

"Great! I'll pick you up at 4:45, and we can go in one car."

"Perfect. But listen, there's something else I have to tell you. I received an anonymous note this afternoon warning me to stay out of the case. It seems our investigating has upset someone who is keeping an eye on us. I turned it over to the police, but we could be in danger. Are you sure you still want to go?"

Cassie was silent for a moment. "I suppose that means we are on the right track. I say we move forward with our plans, anyway. For Andrea's sake."

"I agree. I just wanted to make sure you were okay with it."

"I'll see you tomorrow," Cassie said.

Connie was glad she and Cassie were going alone to the yacht club to try to talk with Nate, especially since she promised Gallagher and Grace that she would keep Stephanie out of harm's way.

As she was hanging up with Cassie, Connie noticed a voicemail from Shannon. What she expected would be an uneventful day regarding the investigation was turning out to be action-packed.

"Hi, Connie, it's Shannon from *Harold's Furniture*. Could you give me a call back when you have a minute? I have some interesting news."

Connie called her right back.

"Hi, Connie, that was quick."

"I was on the other line with Cassie when you called. What's your interesting news?"

"You asked me to let you know if I learned anything else that might be connected to Andrea's death. Well, when I got to work this morning, the recliners that Andrea wanted taken off the floor were no longer there, and I learned that Jeremy was fired yesterday afternoon. I heard from a coworker that Calvin discovered Jeremy was taking a kickback and that was the reason he fired him."

"Wow, so Calvin wasn't behind keeping the recliners in stock?"

"It doesn't appear so. I have to say I'm quite relieved. I hated the idea that my boss could be a murderer. The stress was starting to take its toll."

"You don't suppose Calvin could be scapegoating Jeremy to throw suspicion off himself, do you?" Connie asked.

"I don't think so. I think Calvin genuinely didn't realize what Jeremy was doing. I hear he was pretty ticked off that Jeremy was willing to risk the reputation of the store to make a quick buck on the side. Besides, if Calvin were scapegoating Jeremy, Jeremy wouldn't have left quietly. He apologized to the sales associates, and I heard he looked pretty broken as he was leaving. He was escorted out with a box of personal belongings in hand."

Connie thanked Shannon for the information, and as soon as she hung up, she updated Stephanie and Elyse via text.

Now Calvin no longer has a motive, we're down to three suspects - Cathy, Tori, and Nate, Elyse replied.

Considering Cathy has been lying about her identity, she's on the top of my list, Stephanie said. *I'm glad you and Cassie are going to talk to Nate on Friday and that we're talking to Tori tonight.*

How about if we all meet at Just Jewelry *just before 6:00 tonight? That way we can drive to Tori's together.*

They each replied with a thumbs-up emoji.

Chapter 18

ELYSE AND STEPHANIE arrived downtown at 5:45 and left their cars in the parking lot near *Just Jewelry.*

"I feel strange just dropping in on Tori," Stephanie said as they got into Connie's car. "Maybe we should have looked up her phone number and called first."

"It's better if we take her by surprise," Connie said. "Her initial reaction could be telling, and we'd lose that advantage if we called first."

"I guess I can risk being rude and pushy to find Andrea's killer," Stephanie said.

"Agreed," Elyse said.

The evening had turned overcast, and the lights were on inside Tori's house.

"Oh, good. It looks like she's home," Elyse said.

Stephanie rang the doorbell, and a surprised Tori answered the door.

"Hi, ladies. What are you doing here?"

"We were hoping to talk with you for a few minutes. We have some more questions for you about Andrea."

Tori raised her shoulders, as if she were about to protest, but then she relaxed and stepped back from the door. "Sure, why not? Come on in."

The women entered the house and followed Tori into the living room.

They were surprised to see a woman sitting on Tori's couch. She appeared to be in her early fifties and wore a concerned expression.

"We didn't realize you had company," Connie said. "We'll come back another time. We were hoping to speak with you alone."

Tori gestured for them to sit down. "It's okay. Whatever you have to say can be said in front of Tricia."

Connie wasn't sure whether to proceed. Was Tori trying to throw them off and avoid the conversation?

Fortunately, Tori broke the awkward silence. "This is Tricia Riley. She is my AA sponsor. Over the past ten days, Tricia has come to know me quite well. Whatever you have to say, you can say it in front of her."

Connie took a deep breath. "Okay. We know that you broke into Andrea's house on Monday night and that you were checking her email. We also know that you hit a neighbor's car after having too much to drink and that Andrea knew about it."

Tori glanced over at Tricia, who gave her an encouraging nod.

"I'm not going to deny any of that," Tori said. "I take full responsibility for what I did."

"Do you also take responsibility for killing Andrea to protect your secret?" Connie asked.

"Of course not," Tori said calmly. "I didn't do *that*."

"You had a motive, and Andrea was seen going inside your house with you the morning she was killed. Andrea was inside your house long enough for you to have poisoned her coffee."

Tori's eyes widened. "That's how Andrea died? Someone poisoned her coffee?"

Connie was skeptical that Tori was genuinely surprised.

"She was poisoned with an overdose of Norpramin, which was the antidepressant she was taking," Connie said. "Someone likely poisoned her with the bottle she kept in her purse."

Tori shook her head. "That's horrible. But you have this all wrong. Andrea *was* in my house on Monday morning. We had a long conversation, but it wasn't a disagreement. I was thanking her for everything she had done for me."

"What do you mean?" Connie asked.

Tori continued. "What you said is true. Shortly before Andrea died, I had a really bad night. It all started a few years ago, when someone stole my identity and emptied my bank accounts. In addition to my job as a high school principal, I've been waiting tables on the side to replenish my savings ever since."

Connie remembered that Tori was getting ready for a waitressing shift the last time they saw her.

"I'm not proud of it, but I turned to alcohol to forget my troubles. That night I went to a bar and had a few too many. Fortunately, I made it home in one piece, but I hit the neighbor's car in the process. I passed out in bed but when I woke up and remembered what happened, I felt terrible. I'm ashamed to say that my plan was to say nothing. I justified it by telling myself that the neighbors are rich and I'm struggling financially. And I could have lost my job over it. It turned out to be a blessing in disguise that Andrea saw the whole thing. The next day she told me that she would give me twenty-four hours to tell the neighbor what happened. If not, she was going to."

"You must have been furious," Elyse said.

"I was. I couldn't bring myself to do it. I had hit bottom. I couldn't believe I had put myself in that situation. The following day, I had a long talk with Andrea and explained everything. She said that she would not tell the neighbor if I promised to go to AA. That's why I wanted to thank her on the morning she died. When she came in my house, I told her about my first AA meeting. Tricia was here with me, so I introduced Andrea to Tricia."

"It's true," Tricia said. "I had stopped by before work to drop off a book that I thought might help Tori. I was with Tori the whole time Andrea was here. There is no way she could have poisoned Andrea without my seeing it."

"And if that isn't enough to convince you, I spoke with my neighbor this afternoon and explained everything. I figured, eventually, when I got to the ninth step of the twelve-step program, I would need to make amends, anyway, so I thought I'd get a head start. Fortunately, she agreed not to report it."

Connie was speechless. Not only did Tori no longer have a motive, but if Tricia was with her the whole time she was with Andrea, Tori also had an alibi.

Stephanie gave Tori a warm hug. "I'm so happy that you took this step. It took a lot of courage."

"Thank you. It feels good to get everything off my chest. But just out of curiosity, how did you know that Andrea came inside my house on Monday morning?"

"The cleaning lady told us," Connie said.

"Oh, Allison. She's a sweetie."

"Who's Allison? I'm talking about Cathy Reardon, Andrea's cleaning lady."

"Do you mean the woman who cleaned Andrea's house on Monday mornings?" Tori asked.

"Yes, Cathy."

"No. Her name is Allison Daley. I should know. She used to clean my house until I couldn't afford her anymore."

Connie, Elyse, and Stephanie looked at one another dumbfounded.

"That doesn't make any sense," Connie said. "Why would she be using two separate names for business?"

Tori shrugged her shoulders. "Beats me."

"Well, we've taken up enough of your time," Connie said. "It was nice to meet you, Tricia."

"We'll be rooting for you, Tori," Stephanie added.

As they drove back, Connie wondered aloud. "Why would Cathy use two names for the same business?"

"I don't know, but we should tell the police," Elyse said. "Why don't you do it, Connie? I don't want to admit to Josh that I've been getting involved with his case. Zach won't make a big deal about it, but Josh will make my weekend miserable."

Connie wasn't sure that Zach would be so understanding, either, when he learned she was already back investigating after receiving the threatening note. But she had to do it.

Since she didn't want to give Zach any work-related news when he was probably home for the night relaxing, and since it wasn't time-sensitive, she decided to wait until the following day.

On Friday morning, after filling Grace in on their conversation with Tori, she texted Zach, telling him she had some important news related to the case.

I'll be right over, he replied.

"I was so distracted when I saw you yesterday that I didn't have a chance to ask if your parents got home safely yesterday," Connie said, as she brought out a tray with three cups of coffee for Zach, Grace, and herself.

"They called last night. They made it home safe and sound. I miss them, but it's nice to be able to focus all my energies on the case."

"Are you close to solving it?" Grace asked.

"I can't say we're close to an arrest, but we're continuing to follow leads."

"Well, I might have another lead for you," Connie said. "I spoke with Tori yesterday." Connie decided to leave out the fact that Stephanie and Elyse were with her.

"You just happened to run into Tori, the victim's neighbor, on Thursday evening, when you are normally working?"

"Yes, let's just go with that."

"Connie, you've already upset one person. Can't you just lay low until we make an arrest? I'm worried about your safety."

"I know, Zach. We were just following through with something we had already started. Tori isn't the one we upset. She has an alibi for Monday morning." Connie cringed when she realized she said "we" and not "I." She hoped Zach didn't notice.

"Then you know Tori was with her AA sponsor on Monday morning and couldn't have poisoned Andrea Fontaine's coffee."

"I found that out yesterday. Anyway, we were talking about Andrea's cleaning lady."

"Cathy Reardon," Zach said.

"Yes, but Tori insists that the woman's name is Allison Daley. Tori said that Allison used to be *her* cleaning lady, until she could no longer afford one. I ran internet searches for both Allison Daley and Cathy Reardon, and nothing much came up for either of them. At least not in this area."

"That's strange," Zach said.

"I asked her if she was certain that Andrea's cleaning lady was the same person who used to clean her house, and she said that she had no doubt. She was one-hundred percent certain."

Zach promised to look into it.

Chapter 19

FRIDAY WAS BUSIER than usual, so Connie didn't have as much time to create jewelry in between customers. The day flew by, and before she knew it, Cassie had arrived to pick her up to go to the yacht club for their plans to try to talk to Nate.

"My father said that Nate is always at the bar on a Friday night, so we have a pretty good chance of seeing him," Cassie said as they drove across town.

When they arrived, they claimed an out-of-the-way table with a view of the entire room. Then they went to the bar to order drinks.

Cassie ordered a glass of cabernet, but Connie chose soda water with a splash of cranberry juice and a wedge of lime, since she had to return to work. It was her go-to drink when she wanted it to appear as though she were drinking an alcoholic beverage.

"Don't look now, but Nate just walked in," Cassie said, as they paid for their drinks.

To be discreet, Connie paused before looking. After a few seconds, she turned and took a step toward their table. In her effort to play it cool, Connie hadn't realized that by that point, Nate was right behind her - that is until half of her cranberry juice drink was all over Nate's white polo shirt.

So much for being discreet.

Connie felt her cheeks grow warm as she looked into his brown eyes. She studied his features for a moment. He looked familiar. "I'm so sorry," she finally managed to say, reaching for a cocktail napkin and dabbing the large pink spot on his shirt. But she only made it worse. Now, he had a pink stain with pieces of napkin stuck to it.

Nate looked down at Connie, and she braced herself for a tongue lashing. But instead he appeared entertained.

"Don't worry about it. These things happen," he said with a shrug. He motioned for the bartender to refill Connie's glass, and he ordered a martini for himself.

"Fortunately, I keep a clean shirt in my trunk for when..."

"For when people dump their colorful drinks on your white shirt?" Cassie asked.

Nate chuckled. "Something like that."

While Nate was getting another shirt from the car, Connie paid for his drink as an apology, and she and Cassie went back to their table.

Nate returned a few minutes later with a fresh yellow polo. He went to the bar to get his drink, and the bartender whispered something. Then he walked over to Connie's and Cassie's table. "Thank you for buying my drink, but it was totally unnecessary." He pointed to his fresh shirt. "See? No harm done."

He seems too nice to be a killer.

Since Connie had already blown her chance at quietly observing Nate, she tried the direct approach.

"I really do apologize for my clumsiness. I lost a friend recently, and I've been easily distracted ever since. Perhaps you heard about her murder on the news." Connie looked directly into Nate's eyes. "Her name was Andrea Fontaine."

Nate coughed, spewing some of his drink onto Connie's blouse. This time, it was Nate who grabbed a cocktail napkin and handed it to Connie. He quickly recovered himself. "We've got to stop doing that to each other." His mouth was smiling, but his eyes were blazing. "I did hear about your friend on the news. It's terribly tragic."

"The police will find the killer," Connie said, maintaining eye contact with him. "It's only a matter of time."

He smiled tightly. "I'm sure." Then he joined some friends at another table.

Connie observed him as he drank his martini faster than he probably should have, the sour expression remaining on his face. As soon as he finished his drink, he stood abruptly and left.

"That was interesting," Cassie said. "Did you see the change that came over him once you brought up Andrea?"

Connie nodded. "He was like Dr. Jekyll and Mr. Hyde. He was charming as could be when I spilled the drink on him, then when I brought up Andrea, his demeanor completely changed. I wonder where he went in such a hurry."

"We're not going to learn anything else sitting here," Connie said after Cassie finished her cabernet. "We might as well leave."

When they returned to *Just Jewelry*, Cassie decided to come in for a quick tour of the store. While she was admiring some of Connie's jewelry, Abby, who had been helping a customer in the Fair Trade section, called Connie over to answer some questions about the artisans. People seemed to love learning everything they could about the artists who created the jewelry they were considering purchasing.

While Connie was talking to the customer, Cassie took a seat at the table. When Connie rejoined her, Cassie informed her that she had just texted Stephanie and Elyse to tell them they had spoken to Nate. When they learned that she and Connie were still together, they wanted to come over to hear what happened in person.

About fifteen minutes later, Stephanie, Elyse, Cassie, and Connie were sitting together around the table. Abby popped over in between customers.

She, too, was curious since Connie had been keeping her up to speed on the investigation.

"I can't wait any longer," Elyse said. "How did your conversation with Nate go?"

"Yeah," Stephanie said. "Were you discreet, or did you confront him directly?"

Connie and Cassie looked at one another and laughed.

"I wouldn't exactly say we were *discreet*," Connie said. "We were planning to be, but then…"

"Then Connie spilled a cranberry juice drink all over his white polo shirt."

Stephanie put her hand over her mouth, and the others burst out laughing.

"What did he say?" Abby asked.

"He was actually a really good sport about the drink," Connie said.

"He was a good sport until Connie mentioned Andrea. Then his whole demeanor changed," Cassie said.

"Nate clearly didn't recognize me," Connie said, "so he can't be the one who sent the threatening note. He had no idea we were connected with

Andrea until I said her name. Then he grew angry, gulped down his martini, and left the bar."

"So, you clearly rattled him by saying her name," Stephanie said. "He must be connected to Andrea's death."

"Either that, or he thinks we were referring to the mystery letter that Andrea kept and not the murder. That is, if he's innocent," Connie said. "Nate may not have recognized me, but he sure looked familiar to me. I just wish I knew why."

"Do you think you've met him before?" Elyse asked.

"I don't know. I just feel like I've seen his face somewhere."

"Try not to focus on it," Cassie said. "It will come to you once you stop trying so hard to remember."

As they were talking, Zach walked into the store. He chuckled when he saw all five of them seated around Connie's table.

"I don't even want to know what all of you are talking about, especially since I'm certain it has nothing to do with our murder investigation."

"Can't a group of women get together to talk?" Elyse asked with a smirk.

"They can. But in this case, why do I have the feeling you got together for a specific topic of conversation?"

Connie shrugged "Who knows?"

Zach shook his head. "Actually, it's good you're all together. I did come by to give Connie some news about the case, but you should probably all hear it."

They looked expectantly at Zach.

"We arrested Cathy Reardon today."

You could have heard a pin drop in the store when Zach dropped his bombshell.

Cassie swallowed hard. "*Cathy* murdered Andrea?"

"No," Zach said. "We didn't arrest her for Andrea's murder. But it turns out she is the one who left Connie the threatening note."

Stephanie gave Zach a confused look. "Why would Cathy have threatened Connie if she didn't kill Andrea?"

Suddenly it made sense to Connie. "I think I understand. She wanted me to stop asking questions about Andrea's death, because in our investigation, we discovered that she had two identities."

"More than *two*," Zach said. "She's been moving from town to town pretending to be a housekeeper and stealing bank account numbers and other sensitive information."

"That's how Tori went bankrupt, isn't it?" Connie asked.

Zach nodded.

"I don't follow," Stephanie said.

"Remember how Cathy told us that Tori was her cleaning lady right around the time she lost everything?" Connie asked. "I'll bet Cathy - or Allison or whatever her name is - was the one who stole Tori's identity and caused her all those financial problems."

"That would explain why Cathy didn't have a website or advertise her cleaning business. She was changing her name on a regular basis," Stephanie said.

"And how she could afford a million-dollar home," Elyse added.

"You got it, ladies," Zach said. "Cathy Reardon wanted you to stop investigating, because she was afraid that you'd eventually uncover her secret."

"And we did," Connie said. "When we talked to Tori, she told us that she knew Cathy as Allison. That's when we got suspicious and told you about our discovery. Come to think of it, it was shortly after that that I received the threatening note. We just assumed the note came from the killer."

"The note was from Cathy, but she didn't kill Andrea. Andrea would have been worth more to her alive. She already had all the information she needed to access Andrea's bank accounts and credit cards."

"Are you sure Cathy didn't kill Andrea because she discovered what Cathy was doing?" Elyse asked.

"Andrea didn't know," Zach said. "In fact, Andrea had told Cathy that she no longer needed her services that morning. Apparently, she had really high standards, and Cathy's work wasn't up to them."

So, Cathy was telling the truth about that.

Cassie smiled. "I guess I shouldn't be surprised. Andrea *was* a bit of a perfectionist."

"So far we seem to have uncovered everyone's secrets, except for the identity of the killer," Cassie said.

"The only real possibility left is Nate," Connie said.

"Whether that's true or not, it's time to leave the investigating to the police," Zach said. "There is still a killer on the loose, and he or she is probably getting more desperate."

Connie glanced at the women around her. She guessed they were all wondering the same thing: whether they should tell Zach about Connie's run-in with Nate. But Connie decided not to say anything. Just because Nate reacted strongly when Connie mentioned Andrea's name, it didn't mean he was guilty of murder. His reaction could have been based on the letter Andrea found in the desk.

"Please excuse me, ladies," Zach said. "It's been a long day, and my hammock is calling my name."

After Zach left, Elyse shook her head. "Well, I, for one, am puzzled. All of our original suspects have been eliminated. It wasn't Jason. Calvin no longer has a motive. Jeremy couldn't have done it. Tori was hiding a drinking problem, not a murder. And now Cathy is cleared, as well."

"That only leaves Nate," Stephanie said.

"Or somebody we haven't thought of," Elyse said.

"It can't be," Cassie said. "Andrea was one of my best friends. There's no way she could have had that big of an enemy without my knowing."

"Maybe she didn't know she had the enemy," Elyse said.

"I don't think so," Cassie said. "She led a quiet life. There's just no way."

"But Nate didn't have access to her coffee mug," Stephanie said. "How could he have drugged Andrea?"

Connie let out a deep sigh. "I don't know. That's what we need to find out."

Chapter 20

WHEN A SMALL GROUP of customers came into the store a few minutes later, Elyse, Stephanie, and Cassie left. A woman who appeared to be in her mid-seventies purchased a burnt orange and blue multistrand necklace made by one of Connie's Fair Trade artisans in Kenya, along with a matching bracelet and earrings.

"That reminds me," Connie said to Abby after the woman left. "I don't think we have enough Fair Trade product to get us through the busy season. I'd better place an order with our artisans before it's too late."

"That's a good idea," Abby said. "It's already November, so this will probably be one of your last chances to stock up on merchandise before the snowbirds and tourists return in full force in January."

Connie brought her laptop to the table and emailed Dura with an order, followed by Carmen, her main contact in Ecuador. Both women employed artisans from poor families, and Connie knew they would welcome the business - especially Dura, who was in the process of training new artisans to meet the growing demand that had resulted from Ruby's shop and in *Beach Baby Boutique* carrying some of their items.

"Last week I stopped by Ruby's and *Beach Baby Boutique,* and they both had additional orders that they were hoping would arrive before January," Connie said. She pulled up the note on her cell phone that contained their orders for each artisan. Then she typed them into an email to send to each of her artisans, added her own order, and sent them off.

Just as Connie hit 'send,' her cell phone rang. It was Cassie.

"Hi, Cassie. Long time, no see."

"I know I was just there, but I had to tell you something important. When I got home, Shannon was waiting for me in my driveway. I'm sitting here with her right now."

"Is everything okay?" Connie asked.

"She's a bit shaken up. Calvin offered her an opportunity to move up in the company by training her to take over Andrea's job. Her first training was today, so she worked at Andrea's old desk. Calvin went out to lunch, but Shannon had brought a sandwich, so she stayed in the office. While he was out, she was searching for a file. When she couldn't find it, she looked in Calvin's office. She never found the file, but she did find something else in his desk drawer."

"What did she find?"

"She found a prescription for Norpramin under Calvin's name."

"So, Shannon thinks that Calvin poisoned Andrea with his prescription?"

"Think about it," Cassie said. "It makes perfect sense. Andrea wasn't secretive about the fact that she was taking an antidepressant, so I have no doubt that Calvin would have known. She never hesitated to share her own battle with depression if she thought it could help others. Calvin probably knew that Andrea was taking Norpramin, too. When Andrea went to the restroom, he could have had the pills already crushed and waiting for the opportunity to put them in her travel mug. And the fact that Andrea was taking the same prescription drug as Calvin made it look like anyone who saw her that morning could have poisoned her. Otherwise, he would have been a prime suspect as someone who saw Andrea the morning of her death *and* who had a prescription for the drug she overdosed on."

"I don't know, Cassie. I agree that this gave Calvin the perfect opportunity to kill Andrea, but as far as we know, he didn't have a motive. Calvin wouldn't have pulled the defective recliners off the floor if he killed Andrea over them."

"That's true," Cassie said. "But it seems like too much of a coincidence. Maybe there's another motive we hadn't thought of."

"There could be. Or maybe he pulled the recliners and fired Jeremy to throw off the police. What better way to throw suspicion off himself than to remove his motive?"

"Shannon was pretty freaked out when she found the pills in Calvin's desk. She pretended to be sick and left work right after lunch. She was afraid to be alone in the office with Calvin."

"That's a terrible situation to be in." Connie thought for a moment. "Say, Cassie, does Shannon have a key to the building?"

"Hold on."

Connie could hear Cassie's and Shannon's voices in the background but couldn't make out what they were saying.

"Yes, Connie, Shannon has a key to the main building and to Calvin's office. She said you are welcome to borrow them if you want to get in there and see what you can find. Maybe if you hunt around his office you can figure out if he had another motive."

Connie thought about it. She didn't want to ask Elyse to come, because she would certainly get into trouble with Josh. And Connie had promised both Grace and Gallagher that she wouldn't let Stephanie get in over her head. "I don't think I should go alone."

Connie heard their voices in the background again.

"We'll come with you if you want. Andrea was my best friend, and Shannon said that if we get caught, we'll have a better chance of explaining why we are there if she is with us."

"That's true. We can always say that the three of us were together, and Shannon forgot something in the office when she left earlier today."

"Okay, it's settled. We'll pick you up at *Just Jewelry*. Should we wait until the shop closes, or could you leave now?"

Traffic had dwindled, and Abby was sitting on a stool behind the circular checkout area, located in the middle of the store, reading a school assignment.

"It's pretty quiet here. Abby can lock up."

Within ten minutes, Cassie and Shannon had arrived at *Just Jewelry*.

"You guys be careful," Abby said when they told her where they were going. "Text me when you're leaving the office, so I know you're okay. Otherwise, I won't be able to sleep tonight."

Connie gave Abby a one-armed hug. "Will do."

The three women drove in silence to *Harold's Furniture*. At Shannon's request, Cassie drove them around to the back of the building.

"There's an entrance that leads straight to the offices back here," Shannon said. "This way, we are less likely to be seen."

Shannon unlocked the door and disarmed the alarm system by punching a password into a keypad. Then they entered by way of the hallway leading to Calvin's office. Using the flashlight application on Connie's phone for light, they walked to the end of the hallway and Shannon unlocked Calvin's office.

Connie turned on a lamp instead of the overhead florescent lights, so it would be less evident from the outside that anyone was in there.

Shannon walked over to Andrea's desk and picked up a white sweater that was draped over the chair. "If anyone sees us, I'll just say I was feeling better and came back to get my sweater. Everyone knows I wear it all the time, so nobody would be suspicious."

"What exactly are we looking for?" Cassie asked.

"I don't know," Connie replied. "Anything that might link Calvin to Andrea's death. If he did kill her, we need to know what his motive was."

Cassie began searching Andrea's desk, and Shannon dug around in the seating area in the office suite.

Connie went into Calvin's office and started exploring. She laughed when she saw one of the defective recliners in the corner of his office. *I guess he didn't want to waste them.* They probably weren't dangerous unless someone reclined.

Connie's phone pinged with a text, but she ignored it. It couldn't be that important.

First, she searched Calvin's desk, then the horizontal metal file cabinet on the back wall. She opened the cabinet drawers and glanced through the file folders, but they contained nothing unusual. In frustration, she sat herself down on the chair. "Did you kill Andrea, Calvin?" she whispered to herself.

Connie leaned forward and rested her elbows on the desk. Cassie and Shannon were heading into the office with long faces.

"Any luck?" Connie asked.

They shook their heads.

As Connie let out a deep sigh, her gaze drifted to a photo on Calvin's desk. She picked it up to examine it more closely. It was a family picture. Calvin was looking on, as proud as could be, as two teenage boys steered a sailboat. One of the boys looked familiar. Calvin looked to be about ten years younger, so it wasn't a recent photo. Suddenly, Connie recognized one of the boys. She stared at it for another moment, just to be sure, but there was no doubt about it.

Connie sprang to her feet, with the photo in hand, and bolted across the room. She held it up in front of Shannon. "Who is in this picture?"

"That's Calvin with his wife, Barbara, and their two sons," Shannon said.

"Look," Connie said, showing Cassie the photo. "That's Nate. Nate is Calvin's son!"

Another text came through Connie's phone, but she ignored it again.

Now Connie knew why Nate looked so familiar. She had seen him in a similar family photo, which was displayed in the reception area the first time she was there. Connie could have kicked herself for not realizing it before.

"Oh, my goodness, you're right!" Cassie said. "I never realized Calvin and Nate were father and son."

"I never made the connection, either," Shannon said. "I knew Calvin married into money because of the lifestyle he lives, but I didn't realize that he was married to Barbara Cartwright."

"According to the deathbed letter Andrea found hidden in the desk, Barbara Cartwright is not technically a Cartwright," Cassie said. "Her grandfather was the gardener, not George Cartwright."

"It looks like we found Calvin's motive," Connie said. "It's the same as Nate's. He killed Andrea to keep the Cartwright family secret."

A man's voice floated through the room. "Very good, ladies."

The women looked up to find Calvin leaning against the doorway, holding a gun, and Nate standing right behind him.

Calvin stepped forward. "I told you we couldn't trust these women, son." He waved the gun at Shannon. "Next time you search someone's desk, darling, make sure you put everything back exactly the way you found it."

Chapter 21

CALVIN STORMED INTO HIS OFFICE and yanked the photo from Shannon's hands. "Did you think I wouldn't keep a close eye on you today after you searched my desk and found my bottle of Norpramin? I had a feeling you'd be contacting these two."

Nate followed Calvin into the office and slammed the door shut. "Looks like your instinct was right, Dad."

Calvin waved his gun, forcing the women into a corner, next to the leather recliner.

"I don't understand," Cassie said. "Which one of you killed Andrea?"

Connie took a step forward. "They both did. When Calvin found out that Andrea was going kayaking later that morning, he laced her coffee with a deadly dose of Norpramin. He probably had already crushed the pills and was just waiting until he could get his hands on Andrea's mug. He knew it would take a couple of hours before the drug took effect. So, he had Nate follow her with his boat to ensure that Andrea would die. Nate's the one who whacked Jason with his oar so that he couldn't get help for Andrea."

"They've got it all figured out," Nate said. "What are we going to do with them?"

Calvin went over to his desk, pulled out the bottle of Norpramin, and waved it at Nate. "Let's let them meet the same fate as Andrea. We'll tie them up and take their phones. That way they won't be able to escape before the drug does its job. We can get rid of the bodies early tomorrow, before the store opens."

Nate chuckled. "Brilliant, Dad. They'll never find the bodies at the bottom of the Gulf of Mexico. I know the perfect spot."

Connie didn't doubt that he did.

Calvin handed the gun to Nate, then walked over to a small bar on the other side of his office and poured three glasses of a rich brown liquid. "The pills will go down nice and easy in this brandy." He crushed all the pills in the bottle and added them to the drinks.

"You'll never get us to drink that," Connie said. "And besides, my friends know we're here." Connie had no doubt that her friends would eventually figure out what happened, since she had told Abby where they were going. But at the moment, Connie was more concerned with surviving than with Calvin and Nate paying for their crimes.

"You're lying," Nate cried.

Calvin brought over the glasses filled with brandy and Norpramin and shoved them into the women's hands.

"Don't even think about dumping them on the floor, or I'll shoot you."

It seemed like they stood a better chance taking the pills than being shot.

Another text pinged on Connie's phone.

"Ignore it," Nate said with a wave of the gun.

Connie tried to pretend she was sipping, but this only irritated Nate. "Do you think we are stupid? Drink!"

Connie moved closer to Calvin, and leaned against the desk for support. Cassie and Shannon looked at her with terror on their faces.

Connie gestured with her eyes toward the recliner, but they shot her a puzzled look.

"Hurry up!" Nate cried.

Connie took a tiny sip, then motioned to the recliner again with her eyes.

This time, Shannon caught on to Connie's plan. Shannon threw the brandy and Norpramin into Calvin's eyes, then shoved him into the defective recliner with all her strength. He tumbled back, landing with the chair on top of his chest.

He cried out in anger and Connie took advantage of the commotion to disarm Nate with a reverse crescent kick, a technique she learned in her self-defense classes, and grabbed the gun.

After Cassie freed Calvin from the recliner, Connie forced Calvin and Nate to stand in the corner. She gave Cassie the gun and took out her cell phone to call 9-1-1. To Connie's relief, there were already three text messages from Abby. The third one said, *Your silence is scaring me. I'm calling Zach.* The final text had come in fifteen minutes ago.

Before she could dial 9-1-1, the back door opened, and Connie heard Zach's voice calling out, "Connie, are you up there?"

"We're in here," Cassie yelled before Connie could say a word.

Shannon ran out to greet him and brought Zach and the deputy officer who accompanied him to the would-be murder scene.

*   *   *

On Sunday afternoon, Connie, Elyse, and Stephanie met at the beach as planned to redo the beach day they originally tried to enjoy the day they found Andrea's body. Only this time, they weren't alone. They were joined by Zach, Josh, and Gallagher.

The six friends sat reclining in their beach chairs, which were once again set up around Connie's paddleboard. Even though her friends teased her, telling her she should try to sell the concept to *Harold's*, Connie still thought it made a great makeshift coffee table.

As they relaxed under the sunshine, two kayaks rose and fell on the waves in the distance. When Connie noticed them, she stood abruptly and searched for their drivers.

"Sit down, Connie," Josh said with a chuckle. "I can see the drivers of both kayaks."

Connie plopped back down in her lounge chair and laughed. "I'm afraid every time a kayak drifts by I'm going to be checking for signs of life."

"Well, it certainly won't be from any murders at the hands of Calvin or Nate," Zach said. "Between your statements of what happened on Friday night and the bloody oars we found hidden beneath a false bottom on Nate's boat, the district attorney thinks she has enough evidence to convict both men of murder and attempted murder."

"That's fantastic news," Gallagher said. "But I, for one, can't sit in this hot sun anymore without cooling off. I think I'll go for a swim."

"Sounds like a good plan to me," Stephanie said, hopping up from her chair.

The others followed them into the water, and each couple drifted in their own direction.

As Connie and Zach waded hip-deep, they chatted about the past few weeks.

"Your parents were great," Connie said. "I really enjoyed spending time with them. But I have to admit that I was pretty nervous."

Zach smiled. "I never doubted for a second that they would love you."

"I have a feeling they will get along well with my parents when the four of them have a chance to get to know each other," Connie said.

"What do you mean, 'when they have a chance to get to know each other?' Your parents called my father to thank him for watching out for you when you met with Francis, and apparently they talked for a half hour."

Connie put her hands on her hips. "Are you *serious*? My parents didn't tell me that. What on earth could they have talked about for that long? They've never even met!"

"Who knows?" Zach said. "But they are already talking about planning their next trip to Sapphire Beach at the same time."

Connie smiled at Stephanie and Gallagher when Elyse and Josh waded past them. They were so absorbed in one another's company that they didn't even look up.

"Did we hear you say your parents are coming to town, Connie?" Elyse asked.

"Not that I know of. But our parents are hoping to meet the next time they visit. We think they will get along well."

"Who knows?" Zach said. "Maybe there will be a major event in the not-so-distant future that will bring them together." Zach winked at Connie, then dove into an oncoming wave.

"I told you!" Elyse said to Connie before Zach came up for air. "It won't be long before wedding bells are chiming."

Connie splashed Elyse. "Stop! You don't know that."

But Connie had to admit she was enjoying the idea more than she cared to let on.

The End

Next Book in this Series

Book 9: *Friends, Foes and Felonies*

Paperback bundles are available at Angela's store. Visit:
store.angelakryan.com/collections/paperback-bundles
to save with a bundle.

Individual books are available on Amazon.

OR

Free Prequel: *Vacations and Victims*.

Meet Concetta and Bethany in the
Sapphire Beach prequel.
Available in ebook or PDF format only at:
BookHip.com/MWHDFP

Stay in touch!

Join my Readers' Group for periodic updates, exclusive content, and to be notified of new releases. Enter your email address at:
BookHip.com/MWHDFP

OR

Email:
angela@angelakryan.com

Facebook:
facebook.com/AngelaKRyanAuthor

Post Office:
Angela K. Ryan, John Paul Publishing, P.O. Box 283, Tewksbury, MA 01876

ABOUT THE AUTHOR

Angela K. Ryan, author of the *Sapphire Beach Cozy Mystery Series*, writes clean, feel-good stories that uplift and inspire, with mysteries that will keep you guessing.

When she is not writing, Angela enjoys the outdoors, especially kayaking, stand-up paddleboarding, snowshoeing, and skiing. She lives near Boston and loves the change of seasons in New England, but, like her main character, she looks forward to brief escapes to the white, sandy beaches of southwest Florida, where her mother resides.

Angela dreams of one day owning a Cavalier King Charles Spaniel like Ginger, but isn't home enough to take care of one. So, for now, she lives vicariously through her main character, Connie.

Made in the USA
Columbia, SC
20 May 2024

35934864R00140